BEFORE HE WAKES

MARK ALLAN GUNNELLS

Let the world know:
#IGotMyCLPBook!

Crystal Lake Publishing
www.CrystalLakePub.com

WELCOME
TO ANOTHER

CRYSTAL LAKE PUBLISHING
CREATION

Join today at www.crystallakepub.com & www.patreon.com/CLP

WELCOME TO ANOTHER CRYSTAL LAKE PUBLISHING CREATION.

Thank you for supporting independent publishing and small presses. You rock, and hopefully you'll quickly realize why we've become one of the world's leading publishers of Dark Fiction and Horror. We have some of the world's best fans for a reason, and hopefully we'll be able to add you to that list really soon.

To follow us behind the scenes (while supporting independent publishing and our authors), be sure to join our interactive community of authors and readers on Patreon (https://www.patreon.com/CLP) for exclusive content. You can even subscribe to all our future releases. Otherwise drop by our website and online store (www.crystallakepub.com/). We'd love to have you.

Welcome to Crystal Lake Publishing—Tales from the Darkest Depths.

*To Gabino Iglesias who taught me
the value of the hustle.*

CHAPTER ONE:
THE ACCIDENT

BERNIE WILSON CURSED softly under his breath. The Walmart had ten different checkout stations but only three of them were currently open, the lines at each stretching back half a dozen long. Bernie gripped the handle of his cart, bouncing up and down on the balls of his feet, a kinetic personification of impatience.

He had half a mind to simply abandon his groceries instead of waiting, but the cupboards were nearly bare at home and he didn't want to end up like Mother Hubbard. A supply run was not only necessary but imperative. If he had only himself to worry about, he still may have left, but as it was he had his family to consider. He had to take care of them.

Family.

The word brought a rush of warmth to Bernie's skin, as if his body housed a small furnace somewhere in his gut. Thinking of the love that waited for him at home acted as a balm to soothe his edginess. He took several deep breaths through his nostrils and willed his body to stillness. He had a temper, that had always been one of his greatest weaknesses, but no weakness was so strong it couldn't be overcome. He'd heard that on TV once, maybe an old episode of *Oprah* or possibly *Dr. Phil.* In any case, he recognized it as good advice.

The line inched forward. The cashier, a young woman with the dimensions of a teapot—short and stout—and an unflattering pageboy haircut, seemed the chatty type, engaging each customer in conversation about the weather, the new superhero movie that came out the previous weekend, the sale Walmart had on leaf-blowers, the upcoming Cultural Fair to be held in Greer City Park. Bernie could certainly appreciate good customer service, but when the lines were this long, conversation between cashier and customer should consist of nothing more than, "Good afternoon," and "Have a nice day."

Bernie checked his watch and considered moving to another station. However, neither of the other lines seemed to be progressing any faster, and if he did move then this line was sure to inexplicably speed up. It was one of the unwritten laws of the universe. He scanned the magazine rack next to him, searching for something to occupy his mind and make the wait more bearable. Nothing but trashy tabloids detailing outrageous celebrity behavior, divorces and infidelities, drug addictions and alcohol-fueled brawls. He shook his head and turned away. He didn't even recognize the majority of the faces that graced the covers. He didn't keep up with popular culture these days, hadn't been to a movie in years, and had cancelled his cable subscription some time back. He did occasionally watch old sitcoms from the 1950s on his computer. *Leave it to Beaver, Father Knows Best, Ozzie and Harriet, The Donna Reed Show.*

Wholesome programs that reflected old-fashioned family values.

Feeling a light tap on his shoulder, Bernie turned to the elderly woman in line behind him. She stood slightly stooped, holding a blue shopping basket which contained a jar of spaghetti sauce and a box of noodles.

"Excuse me," the woman said. "I only have two items. Would you mind if I jumped ahead of you?"

"Yes, I would mind," Bernie said and turned his back to her.

Normally he hated being rude, especially to his elders—his mother had raised him better than that—but his tolerance was already stretched thin. He merely wanted to get home, put the groceries away, and have dinner with his family.

He could feel stares of judgment from those nearby at his treatment of the old biddy, but he didn't care. Truth be told, the people around him were mere shadows. All that mattered were the members of his family, and they counted on him. He wouldn't let them down.

Finally, he reached the register and began unloading his groceries onto the conveyor belt. He avoided eye contact with the biddy; she stood uncomfortably close behind him. He refused to feel guilty simply because he put his family ahead of some stranger. He'd been alone for years and thought he was happy, but now that he had a full house, he understood how very empty his life had been before.

"How are you today?" the cashier asked in a perky voice. Her nametag identified her as Kristy, but Bernie thought of her as Teapot.

"Fine," he said in a curt voice meant to convey he had no interest in idle chitchat.

Teapot didn't get the hint. "Did you find everything you needed?"

Bernie nodded, fuming inside that she hadn't yet scanned his first item.

"Do you have any coupons?"

"No," Bernie said, his voice sharper than intended, but the irritation evident in his tone did the trick and Teapot began scanning.

Unfortunately, she didn't stop talking.

"Did you hear about the reward the Barrett girl's parents are offering?"

"What?" Bernie said, wishing Teapot would move faster, work silently.

"You know, the high school girl who disappeared a couple months back. The police have ruled out her boyfriend as a suspect, so her parents are offering ten thousand dollars to anyone with information about what might have happened to her. It's like she disappeared into thin air or something. Kinda scary. I won't walk out to my car alone if it's already dark when I get off work."

A noncommittal caveman grunt was Bernie's only response to this. He took his wallet from his back pocket and pulled out his debit card so he'd have it at the ready. He felt his impatience building again, and as no bagger had come up to the station, he began bagging his own items as Teapot scanned them then placing them back in the cart.

"You're in a hurry, huh?" the cashier said with a pleasant smile.

"I certainly am," Bernie said with a less-than-pleasant tone.

Teapot continued to smile, but the corners of her

lips twitched and the smile took on a strained quality. He could see in her eyes that he'd hurt her feelings, and he was truly sorry for that, but it was her own fault really.

In silence, she finished scanning his items, gave him the total, and he slid his card into the chip reader. He groaned inwardly as he had to decline getting cash back and confirm the total before being allowed to enter his pin. The display screen read "Authorizing" for what seemed a small eternity before finally changing to "Payment Accepted."

He immediately began pushing the cart toward the exit. "Don't you want your receipt?" Teapot called after him.

"Keep it."

He thought he heard the old biddy mutter the word "Bastard" but he kept on going, passing through the vestibule and out the automatic doors. The day was cool but bright, the sun beating down and reflecting off the cars in the parking lot to dazzle the eye. To his right, a card table had been set up and several Girl Scouts were hawking their cheap cookies. A redhead in ridiculous pigtails turned to him as he exited and started her spiel.

Bernie had to admit the cookies looked appetizing, but he could probably order them online and have them delivered right to his door. Every time he had to go out into the world, he always ended up feeling like being a hermit was the ideal mode of existence. He already worked from home, and now that he had his new family, what was the point of venturing out if he didn't need to?

These thoughts preoccupied Bernie's mind as he

looked away from the Girl Scouts and quickly rolled his cart out into the crosswalk. Behind him he heard one of the Girl Scouts shout, then the screech of brakes. From his periphery he sensed an oncoming mass, and he glanced to the right just in time to see the grill of the SUV before it made contact.

At first Bernie felt no pain. Only a sense of weightlessness, a rollercoaster-hollowness in his stomach, as he was lifted into the air. The cart rose with him before it descended onto the hood of a Honda in one of the handicapped spaces, smashing the windshield. Bernie landed on the pavement, the back of his head striking the asphalt with enough force that his teeth clamped together and actually sliced through the tip of his tongue. Before he felt the pain in his right leg, he felt the pain in his skull, bright and explosive like the detonation of a bomb. For a moment he thought hail was falling from the cloudless sky, landing all around him, but then he realized it was only dog food from one of the bags that had been in his cart.

The pain flared, bathing his entire body in a white-hot agony, but then it started to fade. As did the light. Curious, he hadn't realized it was so close to twilight. All around him he heard voices, raised and strident, and though he knew he was the cause of this commotion, he could muster no real sense of urgency.

"Call 911," someone screamed, and Bernie found himself wondering what the emergency was. Had someone been injured?

Oh yes, of course, I have. I was hit by a car.

The light continued to dim. An eclipse perhaps? Suddenly a face loomed over his, an older man with a balding head and a rather bulbous nose. His eyes were wide and panicked. "Oh my god!" the man said. "You just ran out in front of me, I tried to stop but there wasn't time. Don't worry, an ambulance is on the way. You're going to be alright."

Bernie understood all the words the man spoke, but he couldn't quite put them together in a coherent, meaningful way. Who needed an ambulance, and why had no one told him about the eclipse?

The last thought Bernie had before he slipped into unconsciousness was, *My family is waiting at home for me. Who will take care of them if I don't return?*

CHAPTER TWO:
IT'S A BOY

PATRICK YOUNG WANDERED through a dark tunnel, lost and cold and blind. Every so often a brief flash of light would reveal images that he recognized but could not connect in any way that made sense to him. A dirty cement floor, a rusted metal bucket, a water-stained ceiling, a single dim bulb behind a wire cage. He didn't have time to adequately ponder these images because the light flares lasted only seconds and then he was plunged back into utter blackness. Not just an absence of light, but a treatise against the very concept of light. A declaration that light had only ever been a myth, something imagined but not anything real. The darkness was so total, in fact, that he began to doubt he had an actual body, believing that he merely floated in an abyss that had swallowed the world.

And there had once been a world, hadn't there? And he had been a part of it? Yes, he'd been a young man with a rich life, a sophomore in college with a boyfriend he thought he might love, an interest in impressionist art and Middle Eastern food, a fitness freak who liked to lift weights and go hiking.

Or had all that merely been a dream?

Patrick became aware that he'd made his way out of the dark tunnel only when the light started to hurt his eyes. And not a brief flash of light, but a steady frosty glow shed from the bulb behind the wire cage in the water-stained ceiling.

He no longer doubted the existence of his body, either. He'd never been quite so aware of it, in fact. He lay against a cold hard floor, and pinpoints of pain pricked his flesh all over like pushpins stuck in a map. The worst pain was concentrated in his head, a thunderstorm rumbling behind his eyes. He lifted an arm that felt as if it weighed a ton and touched his left temple. His fingers came away tacky with blood.

Patrick pushed himself up to a sitting position, though it took more effort than he would have imagined. The pinpoints of pain became hammer blows, and the room swam and spun around him. He felt vaguely nauseated and the darkness began to reassert itself. He leaned his back against the wall behind him and took a couple of deep breaths to increase his oxygen levels for a boost of energy. Gradually the darkness receded, like shadows fleeing from the rising sun, and his stomach settled. The aches in his body remained, as did the pounding in his head.

Sitting up seemed all the movement of which he was capable at the moment, so while he rested he scanned his surroundings. A small, windowless room, a perfect square that he'd guess to be about ten feet by ten feet. The floor was gray cement, three of the walls—the one at his back, the one to his left, and the one straight ahead in which a heavy-looking door was centered—were rough stone. The wall to his right was blank white plaster. The room was empty except for two buckets sitting next to him. Leaning forward, even that small motion making him feel faint, he looked inside them. One was empty but with dark stains and a foul smell he didn't want to contemplate, the other filled with what looked like dry dog food. Roughly midway down the back wall, a water spigot with a wheel-shaped valve.

Reaching up again, he gently probed the wound on his head, a knot the size of a walnut with an inch-long gash just below the hairline. Even though he barely pressed at the knot, it sent lightning bolts of pain ricocheting inside his skull. What the hell had happened to him?

The last thing he clearly remembered was leaving his dorm room for an early morning jog around Furman Lake. He still wore his gray jogging pants, maroon sweatshirt, and Puma sneakers. He'd taken his usual route, down through the rose garden from the main campus before he started the circle past the dining hall and amphitheater, through the woods then around by the clock tower and Frisbee golf course. He could vividly recall coming up to the large parking lot by the bookstore, because he'd noted how few cars there were that morning, but then everything disappeared into that abyss from which he'd only recently escaped.

Had he been in some kind of accident, maybe slipped and banged his head? That might make sense, except this certainly was no hospital room. Bracing his back against the stone, he slowly pressed his way up the wall until he was standing. The nausea returned and he thought for a moment he would have to use one of the buckets, but gradually the queasiness subsided.

He pushed away from the wall and swayed there for a moment. When it became clear he would not be able to stay up under his own strength, he planted one hand against the stones for support. He began to shuffle to the right, and each step felt unsteady, as if the floor beneath him was unstable and rubbery like one of those bouncy houses for children. He closed his eyes to lessen the vertigo and let his hand trailing the wall lead him. At the corner, he turned and followed until the next corner. Only when his fingers moved from rough stone to smooth wood did he open his eyes.

The door was thick, as thick as the wall surely. He grasped the knob and turned, but the door would not budge. Not even remotely. He rammed his shoulder against the wood several times, but even if he had not felt so weak, he doubted it would have made much difference. The door was solid, the lock sturdy.

Patrick slapped an open palm against the door. "Hello," he called, barely recognizing the husky, quavering voice as his own. "Can anyone hear me? I want out!"

"I don't think he's here right now, but even if he was, he wouldn't let you out."

Patrick whirled around so quickly he nearly lost his balance and toppled to the floor, leaning heavily on the door to keep upright. He scanned the small square again, sure the voice had come from somewhere in the room.

Which was impossible. The area was small and open, no place for anyone to hide. He was alone.

"What's your name?" the disembodied voice said

again, and now Patrick realized it came not from the room but next to the room. On the other side of the plaster wall.

Patrick made his way over, leaving the security of the door to cut across diagonally. His gate was awkward and unsteady, like that of a newborn calf just learning to walk, but he made it without falling. He placed his forehead against the cool plaster and said, "Is there really someone there?"

"Yes, what is your name?"

"Patrick. What's yours?"

"Clare. Are you hurt?"

"Yeah. I think I hit my head or something. I don't really remember. Can you let me out of here?"

A few extended seconds of silence before the reply came. "No, I'm locked in myself."

The pain clouded Patrick's mind, making it hard for him to concentrate or think clearly. He even wondered if he were talking to anyone real or if he were experiencing auditory hallucinations. Could head trauma cause such a thing?

"Are you still there?" the girl asked from the other side of the wall.

"I think," Patrick said and laughed, the sound shrill and brittle. "Where are we?"

"I don't know. I woke up in here, same as you. I haven't been outside of this room since."

"How long have you been with me?" Patrick said then gritted his teeth as if the act of thinking were as strenuous as bench pressing two hundred pounds and tried again. "I mean, how long have you been here?"

"It's hard to say. I don't have a watch, and there are no windows here, so it gets hard to keep track of day and night. Like, right now I have no idea if it's morning, noon, or midnight. As best I can tell, I've been here two or three months."

Patrick turned around so that his back was now against the wall. He let himself sink down until his rear hit the floor. "How did you get here?" he asked, hoping her answer to the question may help him answer it for himself.

"He brought me here. He found me in the park, knocked me unconscious with a baseball bat, and I woke up here."

Indeed, her words brought a revelatory spark of memory. He'd been jogging through the parking lot toward the bookstore. Behind him he'd heard a car door open and a voice call out, "Hey, son!" He'd turned, but that was where the memory began to break down. There had been a figure there, but he couldn't make out any details, and the blur of a long cylindrical object rushing toward his face. Could have been a bat, he supposed.

"How old are you?" the girl asked. What had she said her name was? Caitlin, Connie, Clarice . . .

Clare!

"I'm twenty. How about you, Clare?"

"Fifteen. I'm a freshman at Riverside High."

"That's in Greer?" Patrick asked, finding that the gears in his brain were moving with a little more ease.

"Yeah. I live just off Highway 14."

"I go to Furman in Greenville."

"Greenville, huh? He's branching out. The lady before you was from Greer like me."

"The lady before me?"

"Yeah, there was a woman in that room before you. She was already here when I got here."

"What was her name?"

"Linda," Clare said, then added, "I think."

"You *think*?"

"Well, honestly, she gave me different names on different days, but Linda was the one she gave me most often. I kinda think that was her real one."

"What happened to her?" Patrick asked, not really wanting to know but feeling like he *needed* to know.

"I . . . I don't know. He took her out of here maybe a week ago."

"Took her out? Was she . . . I mean, had he . . . ?"

"She was still alive at the time," Clare said. "I don't know what happened to her after that."

"Did she fight him?"

Silence stretched out for a moment before Clare answered. "No, by that point there wasn't much fight left in her."

Patrick experienced another of those moments where he wanted to avoid asking a question even though he felt the information was vital to his situation. Not yet ready to face the question head-on, he instead asked, "How long had she been here?"

"I don't know for sure. She wasn't very clear on the subject; sometimes she said she'd been here forever. If I had to guess, I'd say a long time. Her mind was pretty much gone after everything he did to her."

He closed his eyes and tried to steady his nerves. He had never been a praying man, didn't believe in divine intervention or deus ex machinas; he believed only in himself, in his own innate abilities, his strength and intelligence and perseverance. If he hoped to find his way out of the nightmare in which he'd awakened, he had to trust in himself. Which meant not lying to himself, not shying away from things that frightened him. These were the very things he needed to face head-on. It was the only way he could hope to figure a way out of this mess.

"What did he do to her?" Patrick asked, his voice steady and sounding more like his own again.

"Well, obviously I couldn't see what was going on, but I could hear plenty. Too much. I tried to cover my ears, but it didn't help. I still hear it in my dreams."

"Hear what? Tell me what he did to her."

"He raped her. Repeatedly and violently. Sometimes several times a day. She would scream and cry and a few times she called my name and begged me to help, but none of that was the worst part."

When she didn't continue, Patrick was tempted to let it go. Did he really want to know the worst part? No, but what he wanted wasn't important.

"What was the worst part?"

When Clare spoke, her voice was soft and tremulous. Patrick had to actually place his ear against the wall to hear her better.

"The worst part," she said after a shaky breath, "was afterwards. The screaming was usually over by then, though sometimes I could still hear Linda whimpering. In the quiet that ensued, I mostly heard what he said to her."

"Was it vile?"

"No, it was sweet. It was tender. After violating her so brutally, he would tell her how much he loved her, how beautiful she was, how happy she made him, how lucky he was to have her in his life. Like they were a pair of newlyweds or something. It was grotesque."

The nausea returned, though for different reasons

this time. Patrick swallowed it down and pushed forward. The more information he could gather, the better. Knowledge was power, as the cliché purported.

"Clare, I don't mean to be indelicate, but has he ever done that to you?"

"No, thank God. I think it would run contrary to his delusion."

"And what delusion is that?"

A creaky, coughing sound came through the wall, and it took a moment for Patrick to realize it was Clare laughing. "He thinks we're his family. Isn't that a riot? He seemed to think of Linda as his wife and me as his daughter. Earlier, when he brought you in, he knocked on the door of my cell and said, 'It's a boy! Congratulations, you have a new brother.'"

Patrick placed both hands on the wall, his head still leaning against the plaster. "Who is this guy, Clare? Do you have any idea?"

"No. I'd never seen him before that night in the park, and I have no idea what his name is. He told me and Linda to call him Big Daddy. Like in that stupid old play we read in English class, something about a cat on a roof. You know the one I'm talking about?"

"*Cat on a Hot Tin Roof* by Tennessee Williams," Patrick said, thinking, *Who cares about the title of an old play from some dead closet-case? We have more pressing matters before us.*

He knew he was being unfair. Clare was just a kid, and she had been through trauma like most people never had the misfortune to know. In that situation, people clung to anything they could to try to keep their sanity from completely fracturing. He'd learned as much in his Psych courses. He'd also learned that in such situations, people had a tendency to lose themselves in their own minds so they didn't have to face the horrors happening to them. That was dangerous, a trap he couldn't allow either one of them to fall into, not if they wanted to get out of here alive.

"Clare," he said, making his voice firm, "I have a motto that's gotten me though life thus far, and I want to share it with you now. I want you to adopt it and make it your own, okay?"

"What is it?"

"No giving up. Pretty simple, I know, but I want you to say it. No giving up."

"No giving up." She sounded uncertain, but at least she'd said it and that was enough for now.

"That's good. No giving up. You just keep repeating that, in your head and out loud. No giving up."

"No giving up," she said again, this time with slightly more conviction.

"Clare, you said he didn't do to you what he did to Linda. Has he done anything to you, anything violent?"

"Yes, he's hit me a few times. Mostly right after I got here, because I'd try to get past him and out the door when he'd come to feed me."

Now we're getting somewhere!

"How often does he come to feed you?"

"It's sporadic. Every couple of days I guess, he comes in with the bag."

"Bag? What bag?"

A pause then, "Do you have two buckets in your room?"

Patrick glanced back at them, a sickening realization dawning. "Yeah, I do."

"One is the toilet, one is the feeding trough. Every

couple of days, he comes in to empty one and fill the other."

"He feeds you dog food?"

"It's doesn't taste so bad, really," Clare said, and he could hear the shame and embarrassment in her voice. "Sort of like dry cereal, at least that's what I pretend I'm eating. Beats starving anyway."

He wanted to comfort her, to assure her she had nothing to be ashamed of, but he needed to get the conversation back on a track that might lead them out of this place. "Clare, you said that you tried to get past him and out the door?"

"Yeah, I even hit him with one of the buckets, but he was just too strong for me. Blacked my eye one time, split my lip another. Said he hated to do it, but sometimes children needed to be disciplined when they misbehaved. He quoted that thing from the Bible about sparing the rod and spoiling the child."

The wheels in Patrick's brain were turning. The asshole that held them prisoner here might be too strong for Clare, but Patrick wasn't a fifteen year old girl.

As if sensing his thoughts, Clare said, "Now he comes with a gun."

"Damn," Patrick muttered, but all hope was not lost. A gun was an unfortunate wrinkle, but not insurmountable. "Clare, do you know what kind of a gun it is?"

"I don't know much about firearms. It's not a shotgun or rifle or anything like that. It's a handgun, maybe a revolver."

"Okay, and can you hear him before he opens the door? Do you know he's coming?"

"Yes. I think we're in a basement because I can hear him coming down stairs."

Good. That was good. If he could hear the guy coming, Patrick could get the drop on him. Be waiting next to the door with one of the buckets, bring it down on the guy's gun-hand as he entered. Risky, but it might work.

Again, showing an uncanny knack for deducing Patrick's thoughts, Clare said, "Please don't do anything to make him mad. He's fucking nuts!"

"Never give up, remember? Say it."

"Patrick, I'm scared that he'll—"

"*Say it!*"

"Never give up." Reluctant, but still she said it which was a good sign. She'd been here for months with only a half-crazy woman to talk to. It shouldn't be too hard to get her to view him as a possible savior. Manipulative, yes, but he couldn't have her crippled by fear. He may need her help at a crucial moment.

"Clare, you said before that you didn't think he was here right now. What makes you think that?"

"Shortly after he brought you in I heard his car crank up outside and pull out. I think the garage or carport might be just above me or something."

"Does he leave often?"

"Not really, not that I'm aware of. He seems to stick close to home, maybe he leaves once a week or something. Like I said, time has gotten a bit wonky for me so it's hard to say for sure."

"When he does leave, how long is he usually gone?"

"Not long at all, maybe an hour. Though he's been gone longer than that this time. I'd say you were out for at least three hours, give or take."

"And when was the last time he filled your bucket?"

"Yesterday, I think. It's still pretty full."

Patrick nodded to himself. He wouldn't say he had anything as solid as a plan, but he had the skeletal framework of one.

"Hey Patrick," Clare said. "Can I ask you a question?"

"Sure," he answered, figuring he'd pumped her for information enough for the time being.

"Do you know if my parents are looking for me? My name is Clare Barrett. Has there been anything in the news about me? I'm afraid my parents might think I ran away or something. We'd been fighting a lot and I'd threatened to do just that."

Clare Barrett . . . something about the name rang vaguely familiar, but truthfully Patrick didn't keep up with local news that much. Or national news, for that matter. This past year, he had developed tunnel vision, his life focused on school and Robert. And the last three months had mostly been focused on Robert, his schoolwork falling a bit by the wayside.

So no, he couldn't say he knew for sure if Clare's name had been in the news, but he figured in this instance deception wouldn't be too great a sin.

"Yeah, there's a manhunt going on for you," he said, the lie rolling off his tongue effortlessly. "Half the state is looking for you right now."

Clare didn't say anything in response, but he could hear her crying softly through the wall.

CHAPTER THREE:
WAITING

OFFICER SANCHEZ STEPPED through the automatic doors into the lobby of the Pelham Medical Center Emergency Department. A bored-looking nurse sat behind a desk straight ahead, alternately reading a paperback and scrolling on her cell. She didn't even glance up at the sound of the doors *whooshing* open. Sanchez scanned the chairs in the waiting area. He saw an Asian couple, the woman cradling a crying toddler; an elderly black man holding a bloody towel to his forearm; a young woman with stringy hair hugging herself and rocking back and forth in one of the plastic seats; and a middle-aged man with a receding hairline and a large nose chewing on his nails. Sanchez walked over to the nail-chewer.

"Mr. Neil Baker?" Sanchez said.

At first, the man continued to stare down at his feet, gnawing at his fingers like a dog with a rawhide bone. He seemed to notice Sanchez's shoes first then let his eyes trail up the officer's legs and torso before landing on his face. "Um, yes, I'm Neil Baker."

"My name is Carl Sanchez," he said and held out a hand. "I'd like to talk to you about the accident?"

Neil shook and eyed the officer's uniform. "I already told the cops who showed up at Walmart everything."

"I know," Sanchez said, taking the seat next to Neil. "I've read the preliminary report, but I have a few follow-up questions."

Nodding, Neil returned to nibbling on his fingernails and staring at the floor.

"So you've been here since they brought Mr. Wilson in?" Sanchez asked.

"Yeah. They wouldn't let me go back with him, but they said they'd let me know how he was doing. I don't know if they've called his family or not."

"Doesn't have any family," Sanchez said. "Lives alone, and my understanding is that all of his relatives are dead."

Neil looked at him, eyes wide and moist. "That's terrible. God, I hope he's going to be okay. I'll never forgive myself if . . . you know, if he doesn't . . . "

While it wasn't Sanchez's job to coddle or comfort, he wasn't a heartless man. He didn't enjoy seeing anyone suffer, which was not without its irony considering his line of work ensured he saw much in the way of human suffering. "What happened was a tragic accident, but it *was* an accident. All the witnesses say he bolted right out into the parking lot without even checking for traffic."

"He seemed to come out of nowhere," Neil said. "I'd stopped at the edge of the crosswalk area, but all I saw were those Girl Scouts selling their cookies. I started forward and then suddenly he was right in front of me. I hit the brakes but he was too close."

"Mr. Wilson is lucky," Sanchez said.

Neil looked at him as if he'd said that it was raining gumdrops. "Lucky? How do you figure?"

"If you hadn't stopped at the crosswalk first, if you'd been traveling at a greater velocity, he would be in much worse shape. Probably lying in the morgue right now instead of the hospital."

"I suppose you're right, but that's little comfort to me right now. You weren't on the scene, you didn't see all the blood. He was still unconscious when they brought him in."

Sanchez remained silent, knowing that nothing he could say would actually ease this man's guilt. They sat quietly for a moment then Sanchez cleared his throat and said, "There is something we need to discuss."

Neil sighed and leaned back until his head touched the wall behind him. "It's about the tickets, isn't it?"

"Yes. You have two outstanding speeding tickets on your record."

"I know, I know. I've been meaning to pay them, I'm sure that's what everyone says, but I mean it. Of course, intentions don't amount to anything if they never become actions. My wife used to say that. She also used to say I had a lead foot, and on that matter she was one hundred percent correct. How much trouble am I in? Should I hire a lawyer?"

"I don't think you'll be charged with anything regarding the accident," Sanchez assured the man. "It seems clear you were not at fault."

Neil looked at him for a moment, one corner of his mouth raised in a humorless half-smile. "But . . . ?"

"But . . . the tickets are an issue."

"Am I going to lose my license?"

"Actually, because you had failed to pay those tickets, you've been driving on a suspended license for about a month."

Neil winced. "What's going to happen to me?"

Instead of answering, Sanchez asked a question of his own. "Do you have the money to pay the tickets?"

"Sure, I have plenty of money. Like I said, I meant to pay, it's just . . . well, I don't have any good excuse which I guess makes it worse, when you think about it."

Sanchez took a moment to consider his options. He'd been told that if Mr. Baker seemed noncompliant or belligerent, he had the right to take the man into custody. However, he didn't think that would be necessary; the man didn't seem to pose any type of threat and he had been through enough today. "I'm not making any promises, but if you can pay the tickets as well as all the fees that have built up, maybe we can reinstate your license and let you off with just points added to your driving record."

"Perhaps I should have my license taken," Neil said softly. "After what I've done, maybe I should be off the roads."

Sanchez placed a hand lightly on the man's shoulder. "Well, you certainly need to slow down on the roads, but I don't think you're responsible for what happened today. Beating yourself up isn't going to change anything."

Neil seemed about to say something when a door opened to their right and a tall man in black scrubs walked out. Not a doctor, Sanchez thought, but maybe a male nurse. Both Neil and Sanchez stood.

The nurse came over to them, and he said to Neil,

"You're the one waiting for word on Mr. Wilson, correct?"

"Yes."

"I'm waiting as well," Sanchez said. "I have a few questions about the accident if Mr. Wilson is conscious."

"I'm afraid not," said the nurse. "The head trauma has caused a cerebral edema, or swelling of the brain. He's in a coma."

Neil sank back into the seat. "Oh God, oh God, oh God!"

"Any ideas how long this coma may last?" Sanchez asked.

"It's hard to say with these types of injuries. Dr. Bice has him on a respirator to keep the blood oxygenated and is pushing hypertonic saline through an IV to help combat the edema. If the swelling does not begin to go down soon, surgery will be our next course of action to relieve the pressure."

"Oh God, oh God, oh God," Neil continued to say like some simple but fervent prayer.

Sanchez handed the nurse one of his cards. "If there's any change, please contact me."

"And I'll be here," Neil said. "I'm not going anywhere for a while."

The nurse left them, and Sanchez sat next to Neil again. "You know, last year my sister's oldest had a bad wreck on a motorcycle."

Neil looked over at him with a slight frown.

"His brain swelled up too," Sanchez said. "He was in a coma for two weeks, and then one day he opened his eyes, looked over at my sister and said, 'Hey Ma, I'm thirsty.' Just like that, and now he's good as new.

Except he's not allowed on a motorcycle again until he's forty."

"Officer Sanchez, I appreciate what you're trying to do, but we both know there are plenty of people who never wake up from comas. I have to start making peace with the idea that I may very well end up responsible for a man's death."

Sanchez recognized this as another of those moments where silence was the best response.

Neil leaned forward, placing his face in his hands, and muttered, "Maybe it's a blessing Mr. Wilson has no family."

CHAPTER FOUR:
PATRICK'S ABDUCTION

THE SUN HAD *only begun to peek up over the horizon, manifesting as little more than a pink line shading to an arch of deep purple, when Patrick Young stepped out of the back exit of Geer Hall. He did a few hamstring stretches in front of the building before jogging off toward the back end of campus.*

He saw no one else as he made his way past the other dorms toward the library, which was precisely why he liked to run so early in the morning, before the campus had truly come to life. He felt that he moved through an empty world, a post-apocalyptic landscape, but instead of leaving him with a sense of loneliness and desolation, there was only tranquility.

Of course, he mused as he ran around the left side of the library, passing the bronze statue of the father with his child propped on his shoulder, there was at least one person Patrick wouldn't mind surviving and sharing this solitude with him. Adam to his Steve.

Patrick had been trying for the last month to convince his boyfriend to join him on these early morning jogs, but Robert insisted he never got up before the sun. In fact, he always arranged his schedule each semester to ensure he never had a class earlier than 10 a.m. He took great pride in that fact.

A smile curled his lips as he descended the stone steps behind the library that led down into the rose garden. The fountain at the back gurgled softly, the cherub holding the large fish with water shooting out of its mouth. As he wound through the labyrinthine pathways of the garden, a small gazebo at the center, the smile lingered, thoughts of Robert causing a tingling in the pit of his stomach often referred to as butterflies, though Patrick thought they felt more like bees buzzing around in there, the vibration soothing and warming.

Patrick and Robert had a lot of differences. Patrick was an early-bird; Robert was a late riser. Patrick liked ethnic cuisine; Robert subsisted almost exclusively on fast food burgers and fries. Patrick appreciated live theater; Robert watched mostly sitcoms and reality TV. Patrick tended to be a bit reserved and quiet; Robert was a blazing ball of gregarious charm and wit. Physically, Patrick was tall and slender; Robert was shorter with a beefy frame. On paper, they wouldn't seem a likely match at all.

Yet when they were together, those differences somehow weren't all that important. What they did share was a wicked, often inappropriate sense of humor, as well as a common core belief in kindness and generosity. Neither of them was particularly religious—though Patrick had an interest in Buddhism and Robert still identified as Christian—but they both strove to lead ethical, moral lives. They agreed on all the things that truly mattered.

Not to mention the fact that the sex was phenomenal.

Patrick ran down the path that led out of the garden, the lake spread out before him like a pool of dark ink. The rising sun glinted across the surface of the water like golden highlights. He turned to the right and jogged down toward the dining hall, the school's distinctive clock tower looming in the distance like an accusatory finger pointed at God. At this hour, breakfast was not yet being served, but through the glass of the rotunda he could see workers preparing the morning's meal. He slowed slightly, remembering when he had first met Robert inside.

It had been lunchtime, and Patrick had been having a rare meal on campus as he did a little last-minute cramming for a Physics test the next day. A shadow had fallen across his book, and he'd looked up to find a stranger standing by his table, smiling at him from behind round, wire-frame glasses.

"Can I help you?" Patrick had asked when the man said nothing.

"Didn't I see you at the production of Hairspray *last month?"*

Patrick nodded. "I was there. It was pretty good, wasn't it?"

"I guess, if you're into that sort of thing. My Public Speaking professor made the whole class go. Can you believe that, forcing us to go to a play? Crazy, right?"

"I agree. I can't imagine why someone would have to be forced to go to a play?"

The man had shrugged and sat down across from Patrick without waiting to be asked. "Let's just say I've known a lot of fat chicks in my life—I mean, I'm gay, they're just sort of drawn to me—and none of them break into song that much."

Patrick had found himself laughing despite himself. Normally he hated being interrupted while studying.

"I'm Robert, by the way," the man said, holding out a hand.

Patrick shook and gave his name.

"You were at the play with Gary Edwards, weren't you?" Robert had asked.

This unexpected question had caused Patrick to stammer and fidget in his seat as if it were a bed of hot coals. He and Gary had dated for about three months, the relationship imploding in spectacular fashion only the previous week when he'd discovered Gary had been cheating on him with several different guys.

"That's over," Patrick said curtly, staring down at the book so he didn't have to meet the other man's eyes.

Robert had started laughing, causing Patrick to glance up. "Whew! That's a relief. I was kind of dreading having to tell you to drop-kick that loser to the curb, because he'll stick his dick in any warm hole."

"Yeah, well, I already figured that out for myself. A little later than maybe I should have, but I eventually got the memo."

"Gary and I dated briefly last semester, until I found out he'd slipped it to my friend Samantha. My ex-friend Samantha, I should say."

"Samantha?" Patrick had said so loudly several people at nearby tables looked their way. "He never told me he was bi!"

"As I said, any warm hole. He's not picky."

"Somehow that doesn't come as much of a comfort to me."

"Look at it this way," Robert said with a wide, bright smile, "at this rate he'll have worked his way through the entire student population of Furman by midterms and then maybe he'll transfer to some other school for fresh meat."

The wounds from the breakup had still been open and raw, but despite this Patrick had found himself returning Robert's infectious smile. "Maybe he could transfer to Bob Jones University. Those ultra-religious students might give him more of a challenge."

"Nah, I've hooked up with my share of guys from Bob Jones myself. The repressed types are usually the easiest to get out of their pants."

They had shared a laugh, then settled into a silence that was a bit awkward but not entirely uncomfortable. Finally Patrick said, "Thanks for trying to save me. I appreciate the thought."

"No problem, and hey, if you aren't busy tonight maybe we can have dinner and see a movie."

Patrick had found himself wanting to say yes, which was rare. He usually didn't like to make decisions impulsively. "Maybe some other time. I have an exam tomorrow, and I really have to get in some more study time."

"How about we nix the movie and just go out for dinner? An hour or two, tops, then I'll deliver you to your dorm so you can get right back to the books."

Intellectually, Patrick knew he should say no. He had even enumerated the reasons in his mind. 1) He really did need to study for this Physics test. 2) He was fresh from a bad breakup and didn't need to jump into anything new until he had time to heal and process. 3) He didn't know anything about Robert other than they'd both dated the same man and Robert occasionally hooked up with closet-cases from the Christian college in town. 4) He wasn't even all that attracted to Robert physically. The man was a bit thicker than Patrick usually went for, his hair unkempt and his clothes wrinkled, giving him an altogether sloppy appearance.

All those reasons had been true and undeniable . . . yet he still found himself saying yes. Even now, months later, he couldn't explain the pull he felt to Robert. It went beyond words or even reasoning. It was instinctual and primal. While Patrick read a lot of Buddhists texts, he wasn't sure he believed in the concept of reincarnation, but the strongest proof he knew was that instant sense of kinship with Robert; surely they must have known one another in a past life.

He had gone out to dinner with Robert that evening, but he didn't return to studying afterwards. They'd spent the night together, and almost every night since then. Patrick had made a C on that Physics exam, beginning the downward slide of his grades. He wasn't in danger of flunking out or anything, but he hadn't seen an A or a B since meeting Robert. What may have seemed to the outside observer as a rebound had turned into the most intense relationship of Patrick's life.

He turned by the fraternity housing and passed the clock tower on his left. He picked up speed as he ran past the amphitheater and the path rose up into a wooded area. Patrick pumped his legs, enjoying the feel of the cool sweat coating his body as well as the burn in his calves as he made his way up the steep incline. When Patrick had started Furman, this particular hill had been nearly impossible for him; halfway up he'd usually have to stop, catch his breath, then walk the rest of the way to the top. He hadn't given up—"No giving up" was his motto, he'd actually had it printed up on a T-shirt he sometimes wore to the gym—and now he made it up the hill without even getting winded.

The trail curved around and sloped downward on the far side of the lake. As Patrick started the descent, he hinged forward at the hips, resisting the urge to lean back and instead gradually moving his center of gravity forward as he picked up speed. A lot of people thought of uphill running as the most strenuous, but downhill running could be just as strenuous and often left a person even sorer due to the eccentric contraction of the quadriceps and lower leg muscles.

At the bottom of the hill, he began to sprint, pounding over the stone bridge that arched like something from a fairytale. He passed a power-walker going in the opposite direction, a middle-aged woman who smiled and nodded at him. Patrick smiled and nodded back.

When he reached the small brick building that housed restrooms, he stopped to relieve his bladder and hydrate at the water fountain out front. He trotted over to the edge of the lake, staring across the water toward the main campus. The sun had climbed higher over the horizon, reminding Patrick of a baby crowning. The water shimmered as if bejeweled, flocks of ducks and bevies of swans cutting across the surface, the wake of the fowl creating V patterns behind them, their honks sounding almost like laughter.

Patrick laughed along with them, feeling buoyed by a sense of contentment that was almost alien to him. He didn't think of himself as an overly pessimistic man, but neither was he a wearer of rose-colored glasses. He often called himself a pragmatist; life was neither a pit of despair nor a bowl full of cherries.

Yet, at the moment, he felt as if his bowl were overflowing with maraschinos. He was in the best physical shape of his life; he was in a relationship with someone he was crazy about and who was crazy about him; while his grades had dropped, he was still passing all his courses; even his parents were coming around.

When he came out to them on his seventeenth birthday, in rather dramatic fashion—he blew out the candles on his cake and then told them he'd wished for a boyfriend with a stud in his tongue—they had reacted not with outright disapproval but with guarded reservations. He came from a family of progressive-minded people who supported gay rights but in an abstract sort of way. Discovering they had a gay son put his parents' convictions on the subject to the test. He'd never introduced them to anyone he was dating . . . until Robert. Last month his parents had come down for a weekend visit, and much to Patrick's delight, Robert charmed them with an ease that seemed effortless. Before leaving to return home, his mother had pulled Patrick aside and told him, "You've got one of the good ones. Don't mess this up."

Walking back to the paved path, he resumed his jog, running the rest of the way around the lake. He reached the large parking lot in front of the bookstore, bending first his left leg back, grabbing the foot and pulling it up behind him, then repeating the process with his right leg to stretch out the quads. The lot was nearly deserted this early on a Sunday morning, only four vehicles. Two compact cars, one pickup, and one SUV. The SUV was running, exhaust spilling from the tailpipe like a smoke machine.

Patrick cut across the parking lot, intending to go back through the rose garden and up by the library again. His thoughts turned to Robert again, as they always seemed to these days. He'd finally convinced Robert to go with him to see the Greenville Symphony at the Peace Center. They had tickets for next Saturday, and they were going tomorrow afternoon to be fitted for tux rentals.

Patrick was imagining how dashing Robert would look in a tuxedo as he passed the SUV. Dimly, he heard the driver's side door open but he didn't pay it any attention. Only when he heard a voice behind him shout, "Hey, son!" did Patrick pause and turn. He saw the man standing there, holding a baseball bat in his hands, but he felt no immediate sense of danger. This was Furman, not only one of the most beautiful campuses in America but also one of the safest. Besides, the man had a pleasant smile on face, nothing to indicate malice or ill intent.

"Can I help—?" Patrick began, thinking perhaps the man was looking for the baseball field, but then *the man swung the bat like he was going for a homer. Patrick had time to muse that the man's facial expression remained placid and friendly, but then the bat connected with the side of his head and he fell into a yawning, dark abyss.*

CHAPTER FIVE:
EXPLORING THE ENVIRONMENT

PATRICK SAT IN the far corner with his head against the plaster wall. Halfway along the back wall sat the bucket filled with dog food, just to the left of the spigot. The empty bucket he'd placed all the way in the opposite corner.

Only it wasn't empty any longer.

He'd held out as long as he could, but eventually it had been go in the bucket or in his pants. Both options were humiliating, but he went with the one that would allow him to keep at least a tattered shred of dignity. Clare must have heard, just as he'd been able to hear her when she went earlier, but she had the tact not to say anything. In fact, they hadn't spoken since, as if perhaps she was sensitive to his discomfort and embarrassment. Or maybe she'd simply fallen asleep.

Now that he had eliminated, his body told him it was time to fill it back up again. His stomach cramped and gurgled, the hunger pains starting out as mere twinges but gradually building to sharp jabs. He hadn't eaten anything since dinner Saturday night, twenty-four hours ago. Or possibly even longer than that, he had no real way of knowing. All he knew was that he was voraciously hungry and he had no way of satiating the hunger.

His eyes strayed to the other bucket, the one filled with dog food.

Dog food, not *people* food, he kept reminding himself.

It doesn't taste so bad, really. Sort of like dry cereal . . .

Patrick shook his head, both in negation of the thought and to clear his mind. He'd already been reduced to shitting in a bucket; he would be damned if he'd eat dog food like some mongrel. He thought he'd read somewhere that a person could survive up to three weeks without food. Only about a week without water, so thank God for the spigot.

Of course, the pragmatic part of his brain said, he had to keep his strength up. If he hoped to gain the upper hand against whoever had abducted him, he couldn't allow himself to get so malnourished that he lacked the strength to fight.

It's only been a day, he told himself. *Yes, you're hungry, but that's all it is. You aren't starving. Think of it as a fast. Sure, if this goes on long enough the time may come that you'll have to put aside your dignity and do what has to be done . . .*

"But not yet," he muttered.

"Did you say something?" Clare asked, her voice so close he guessed her head rested almost in the exact spot as his on the other side of the wall.

Not wanting to admit he'd been talking to himself, Patrick said, "Do you think he's still gone?"

"I haven't heard the car so I think so."

"How long do you figure it's been?"

"A long time, longer than he's ever been gone since I got here. You don't think . . . ?"

"What?"

When Clare spoke again, her voice was like that of a girl half her age, lost in a large department store and unable to find her Mommy. "You don't think he'd just leave us, do you?"

The question hit Patrick like a brick to his face. He'd been so focused on the imagined confrontation between himself and the man whose face he couldn't quite remember that it had never occurred to him that the creep might never come back. That he would simply abandon them here to die like hamsters left in a cage when the family goes away for vacation.

This notion had a ripple-effect of ramifications. Their captor wouldn't necessarily even have to abandon them willingly. What if he went out somewhere and had a heart-attack? Or was blindsided by a drunk driver running a traffic light? Or fell off a cliff, was bitten by a rattlesnake, mauled by rabid dogs?

"It hasn't been long enough to worry," he said, as much to quell his own budding panic as to assure Clare. "We don't know anything about this man or what he does. There are a million reasons why he might be gone longer this time. You said he thinks of us as his children, that he's building a family in his sick mind. He wouldn't leave his kids behind."

"Are you sure?"

"Positive," Patrick said with more conviction than he felt.

Clare let out a shaky laugh that dissolved into a

sob. "I feel like I'm losing my mind, like I'm becoming a split personality or something."

"What do you mean?"

"It's like I'm two people. One of them hopes the bastard never comes back, but the other is afraid that he'll never come back. I can't decide which possibility is worse."

Not coming back, that's worse, Patrick thought but didn't say. If he didn't come back then they were trapped with no hope of escape. But if he came back, that gave Patrick a chance. A chance to overpower the creep and save both himself and Clare. And this Linda if she was still in the house and not buried in a shallow grave somewhere.

So yes, Patrick definitely wanted "Big Daddy" to come back, but he also had to seriously consider the other option. If they had been discarded here like so much trash, no one was going to save them but themselves. Clare was a kid, and one balancing on a thin wire above a pit of despair and madness, and Patrick suspected her foot was slipping. That left their survival up to him. Quite a responsibility he didn't ask for, but he had no plans to die. Not here, not like this, so he had to act.

Pushing himself to his feet, he cast a scrutinizing eye about the room. He went to the door and tested it again. Glancing upward, he estimated the ceiling was about twelve feet above the floor, constructed of wooden planks. They looked solid as well, but he'd never be able to reach that high without something more than two rusty buckets to stand on.

"Hey Clare," he said. "I know this is a longshot but I don't suppose you have any windows in your room?"

"No, I think we're underground. Just walls and a door."

"And all your walls are stone except the one that separates us?"

"That's right."

Patrick mulled this over for a moment. Obviously their cells had once been one long room, and the plaster wall had been added to divide it into two. He began to make his way slowly to the left, pressing on each individual stone from the floor to the utmost height of his reach, looking for any that might be loose or wobbly.

"What are you doing over there?" Clare asked.

"Just exploring the environment."

"Please, Patrick, don't get us into trouble."

He paused and glanced back toward the plaster wall, imagining he could almost see the shape of her crouching on the other side, hugging herself and trembling. "Clare, listen to me. We're already in trouble. *Serious* trouble."

"I know, but...you can make it worse. Trust me, you can make it so much worse."

Patrick felt a sharp retort rise to his lips, but with a grimace he swallowed it back down like a horse pill. He had to remind himself that Clare had been here for months, had suffered beatings and had to listen to the woman in the cell next to her being violated. Had been reduced to eating dog food and relieving herself in a bucket. As dire as their circumstances were, he still needed to be patient and sensitive, not push her too hard lest she break completely.

Making an effort to soften his voice, he said, "I know this bastard has hurt you, but he will keep on hurting you unless we find a way out of here."

Silence for a moment, then the sound of quiet sobbing. "I'm just so afraid."

"I know, and I'm afraid too."

"At least you're a boy, you don't have as much to be afraid of."

"What do you mean?"

"I worry that . . . well, with Linda gone now, what if he decides to upgrade me from daughter to wife?"

This shocked Patrick into speechlessness for a moment. He was reminded again of how much more women had to fear in life than men. Yes, he was aware that men could be victims of sexual violence, especially in the gay community, but statistically women were much more likely to be targets. He'd had female friends tell him it was something they thought about almost every day. He could empathize but he couldn't ever really understand, not completely. Even here, with him and Clare in the same boat, she harbored fears he hadn't even considered.

"All the more reason for us to find a way out," he said lamely.

Clare didn't respond to this, other than more hiccupping sobs.

Patrick resumed his systematic search for weaknesses in the walls. Though the room wasn't particularly large, there were so many stones. He knew this would take quite a while, but what did he have if not time?

He tested each stone, even running his finger around the mortar in between to see if any of it was crumbly. It took him almost twenty minutes to reach the corner and begin on the next wall. The closer he got to the bucket he'd used earlier, the more the unpleasant smell assaulted him, making him want to retch. He resisted the urge, taking shallow breaths through his mouth, because he knew if he vomited it would only make things worse.

Patrick found himself flashing back on his time dating Gary. Gary had tried several times to convince Patrick to go to one of those Escape Rooms, where you paid to be locked in a room and you had to search for clues and solve puzzles to free yourself in a set amount of time. Gary had thought they were tremendously fun and exciting, but Patrick had had zero interest. He didn't like murder mysteries, brain teasers, or even the game Clue.

Now a part of him wished he had given in to Gary, thinking that perhaps he could have gleaned some skills from such an experience that might help him now. Of course, the Escape Rooms were manufactured to be solvable; there was no such guarantee in this situation. There were no clues, no puzzles to figure out.

Still he kept going around the room, testing the stones, almost as if one might push inward, a hidden switch that would open that door and he'd get a prize for his troubles.

As he worked his way down the long back wall, he spent extra time around the spigot, grabbing the cold metal faucet and pulling, pushing, yanking, and jerking, but the thing didn't budge.

"Patrick, why are you so quiet?" Clare asked suddenly, startling Patrick so badly that a squeaky gasp escaped him. He'd been so caught up in what he was doing that he'd nearly forgotten about the girl.

"Clare, honey, I'm kind of busy right now."

"Just talk to me. *Please.* So I'll know you're still there."

"Doesn't look like I'm going anywhere."

"I need to hear your voice. I need to know I'm not alone. Even if I can't see you, your voice keeps me grounded. It helps, at least."

Patrick came to a stone, about three feet up the wall, with a deep maroon stain darkening it. He ran his fingers down the rough surface and they came away dry. Could have been blood, but there was no way to be sure. He felt suddenly lightheaded, and he squatted down, head hanging, waiting for his equilibrium to return. Perhaps it wasn't only the girl who needed some grounding.

"What do you want to talk about?" he said, resuming his progress around the room's perimeter.

"I don't know. Anything. What's your favorite TV show?"

"Um, *Game of Thrones*, I guess."

"Yuck! Too violent for me. I like *Riverdale*."

"Isn't that the one loosely based on the *Archie* comics?"

"I don't really know what that is."

"Such a baby," he said, though she was only a few years younger than him. "Were you also one of those girls who went crazy for *Twilight*?"

"I thought the movies were okay. Never read the books."

"Not much of a reader?"

"Not really. I mean, when I was really little, I read the *Harry Potter* series. Well, the first few anyway. They got kind of long and involved after a while."

Patrick had made his way back to the corner of the

back and plaster wall. He let his fingers trail along the plaster and he took up his investigation again, working his way back toward the door.

"So, what's your favorite subject in school?" Patrick asked.

"I guess I used to like math alright. I've got a head for numbers."

"*Used to* like math? Why the past tense?"

"Well, I haven't been doing too great in any of my subjects the last year. Not since I started dating my Hank."

"I can relate to that more than you know."

"What are you majoring in at Furman?" Clare asked.

"Psychology."

"That's cool. So you want to be a psychologist?"

"I have no idea what I want to be," Patrick said, something he hadn't really admitted out loud to anyone. "I'm interested in a little bit of everything. I went undeclared until recently when I was told I *had* to declare one. I picked the subject I liked best, but I'm still trying to figure out exactly what I'm going to do with a Psych degree once I'm out of school."

"My friend Brianna's older brother has a Psych degree. He works with the mentally handicapped. A case worker or something."

"Well, that's an option. I'll probably end up as a barista at Starbucks or something."

"At least, you'll get a discount on those expensive drinks."

Patrick found this conversation surreal, like earlier when they'd briefly discussed *Cat on a Hot Tin Roof*. A discussion of favorite subjects and majors, as if they weren't prisoners in this hellhole. Again, he reminded himself that this was a coping mechanism, and it was in his best interest to help Clare cope.

"So, you and this Hank serious?"

"Yeah, I never met anyone quite like Hank. My parents hate him, though."

"He a bad boy?"

"Not at all. They say they don't like him because he's too old for me."

"What are we talking? Forty-five, fifty?"

This elicited a weak, sputtering laugh from Clare. "He's eighteen, only three years older than me. That's not the real reason they don't want me dating him, though I know they'll never admit to it."

"What's the real reason, do you think?"

"His family is from Niger. They're Muslims."

"A Muslim named Hank?"

"It's a nickname. His real name is Haneef."

"Well, in the current political climate, a lot of people are feeling iffy about Muslims."

"It's not fair to judge him by his parents' religion. Hank doesn't even believe any of that crap."

Patrick had made his way back to the door. He had found no weaknesses in any of the stones, not even anything small enough to give him a sliver of hope. The only weakness he'd found anywhere in the room was the plaster wall, but even if he could get through it, he'd only end up in another cell. One of those out of the frying pan, into the fire situations. He slumped to the floor, exhaustion seeping into his bones now that his little project was finished.

Exhaustion and hunger. His stomach rumbled again, the sound of distant thunder forewarning of a storm on the way.

Clare continued to chatter away about religious intolerance, but Patrick tuned her out, retreating into his own thoughts. He estimated it had taken him nearly an hour to go around the entire room, and it had probably been at least five or six hours since he'd awaken here. Clare had guessed he'd been unconscious three hours. So approximately nine hours since he'd been brought here, nine hours since his abductor had left the premises.

"Clare," Patrick said when the girl paused to take a breath, "did Big Daddy say anything to you before he left this time?"

"I told you he—"

"I mean other than the 'It's a boy' thing. Think, did he give you any indication where he might be going that would take him longer this time? Even something like, 'See you tomorrow' or 'It's been nice knowing you.'"

She was quiet for a moment, apparently scouring her memory banks. "No, nothing. He told me I had a new brother then I heard him go back up the stairs. A few minutes later the car started up and he was gone. I assumed he'd be right back like all the other times."

"Damn it," Patrick murmured. He stood and walked back across the room, stopping at the spigot. As another sharp hunger pain jabbed at his abdomen, he looked down into the bucket, happy to note that the dog food looked unappetizing, the smell of it making him wrinkle his nose in disgust. He knew if this went on long enough, that would change and the dog food would start to look and smell like a four-course meal in a swanky restaurant.

Ignoring the bucket for now, he hunkered down

and twisted the spigot's valve. Cold water gushed out in a torrent, splashing the floor and creating a puddle. He cupped his hands under the spray and brought the water to his lips, gulping it down. He figured if he filled up with enough water, that might help stave off the hunger for a little longer.

"That sounds good," Clare said, a note of longing in her voice.

Patrick shut off the flow, wiping his dripping hands on his pants. "What's that?"

"The water . . . sounds good. Bet it tastes good too."

"A little metallic but beggars can't' be—" Patrick stopped speaking abruptly, his mouth snapping shut with an audible *click* of his teeth. He looked down at the water that had pooled on the floor, spreading out to create a puddle that darkened the cement. "Clare, do you have a spigot over there?"

Another laugh, this one devoid of humor. "No, that's an amenity only available in your suit."

"But you can't have gone without water for all the time you've been here. What have you been drinking?"

"Big Daddy put a large thermos in here. He usually fills it up when he fills my bucket."

"You may have to ration for a bit," Patrick said. "How much do you have?"

"Nothing. I drank the last of it yesterday."

CHAPTER SIX:
MISSING PERSON

ROBERT MCAFEE SAT up in bed, on top of the covers still wearing his clothes from the day before, as the window across from him lightened with the dawn of a new morning. His cell phone was nearby, and every few minutes he picked it up and checked Patrick's Facebook, Twitter, Instagram, hoping for some new post, anything to indicate Patrick still existed in the world and hadn't simply evaporated into the atmosphere.

Nothing. The last appearance from Patrick on social media was a Tweet from two days ago that simply read, "Enlightenment comes not from denying your emotions but from understanding them." He'd concluded with the hashtag #BuddhaKnowsBest.

Robert smiled as he read the Tweet for the zillionth time. It was exactly the kind of philosophical-sounding nonsense his boyfriend loved to post online. Robert often teased him about it, calling him Dali Lama. Not with any spite, but with good-natured affection. The way Patrick sometimes called Robert Mr. Sloth. Not traditional pet-names like sweetheart or honey, but said with the same degree of love. He even found it endearing the way Patrick never used text-speak but all his posts were in complete sentences with full punctuation and no abbreviations.

Pulling up his own Facebook page, Robert began scrolling through all the pictures he'd uploaded the last few months of him and Patrick. Taken on campus, at Falls Park, their trip to Asheville, the Greenville Zoo, the Upcountry History Museum. Always with their arms around each other, cheeks pushed together. As different as the two men were physically, in all the photos they wore identical high-wattage smiles.

Robert was startled by the beeping of his roommate's alarm at seven. With a slap of the hand, Kirk silenced the alarm, broke wind with a sound like paper ripping, then swung his feet out of bed. After a stretch and a yawn, he glanced over at Robert. "Dude, have you been up all night?"

Robert only nodded in response.

Kirk stumbled over to his closet and rummaged through the clothes that littered the floor, smelling some and discarding them, before coming up with a wrinkled shirt and a tattered pair of cargo shorts. Grabbing his travel bag of toiletries, he started for the door to head to the floor's communal bathroom. He paused with his hand on the knob and looked back at his Robert. "So you still haven't heard from Patrick, huh?"

Robert shook his head.

Kirk fidgeted, shifting from one foot to the other like he urgently had to relieve his bladder. "He's probably just sick or something. I'm sure he'll be in touch today."

With that, Kirk left the room quickly, almost as if he were fleeing the scene of a crime.

Robert still marveled at the fact that he'd confided in his roommate at all. They weren't exactly friends. No animosity or disdain, but neither was there camaraderie or bonding. They didn't hang out together and rarely spoke more than a few words to one another in a given day. Sometimes, Robert thought it was like living with a benign ghost. Objects moved around and you heard noises from time to time, but no real interaction.

Truth be told, Robert had few actual friends. He had acquaintances by the dozens, but the only person he'd let get truly close was Patrick. With no one to tell about his worries, he'd turned to Kirk and unburdened last night. Such raw intimacy clearly made his roommate uncomfortable, but Kirk had made a commendable if lackluster effort at being sympathetic.

Robert tried calling Patrick again. Like all the times before, the call went straight to voicemail. Disconnecting, he sent another text. The latest in a string of texts over the past twenty-four hours that had gone unanswered.

"Where R U? Did I do something wrong? R U mad at me? Please say something I'm worrying myself sick over here."

He waited five minutes, and when there was no response he sighed and got off the bed, stepping into his shoes. He left the dorm room, not bothering to shower, or brush his teeth, or even run a comb through his hair. It wasn't as if he planned on attending any of his classes today anyway.

He exited Manly Hall and followed the walkway to

the stone steps that led up to the next series of dorm buildings. Geer Hall was the next dorm up the hill. Robert didn't have a keycard to get into this building, so he waited outside the door until someone came out, a girl in a pink jogging suit, hair in a ponytail, and a backpack slung over one shoulder. Robert said good morning to her then slipped in before the door closed all the way.

Patrick's room was on the second floor, and Robert pounded on the door for several minutes, until his knuckles ached and began to abrade from the rough grain of the faux wood. He turned when he heard a door behind him open. Paul Guffey came out of the room directly across the hall and nodded at him. The two shared a Statistics class this semester.

"Hey, Robert."

"Have you seen Patrick?" Robert asked without returning the greeting.

Paul paused for a moment tilted his head as he mulled over the question. "I think the last time I saw him was day before yesterday. Yeah, Saturday, that's right."

A bottomless pit opened in Robert's gut and it felt as if he were turning inside out and falling into it. "I haven't heard from him since Saturday night."

"Maybe he had some kind of family emergency and had to split."

"I guess that's possible."

"I have to run or I'll be late for Bio. See you in Statistics tomorrow."

"Yeah, see you then," Robert said, though he had no real intention of going to his classes tomorrow either, not until he figured out what was going on with Patrick.

Alone in the hall again, Robert leaned his forehead against Patrick's door and felt tears making hot trails down his cheeks. Worry twisted through him like coils of barbed wire, shredding his insides.

Everything had seemed normal Saturday. They'd had an early dinner at Pita House; Robert marveled that he was actually growing to like the taste of hummus and falafel and even those stuffed grape leaves. They'd made plans to go to Men's Warehouse across from Haywood Mall and get fitted for tuxes Monday night.

Tonight. We're supposed to be there at six tonight.

They had decided not to spend the night together—Robert had taken to spending most nights in Patrick's room since Patrick had a single with no roommate—because Patrick was adamant that he needed to get some serious work done on a paper for Abnormal Psych. Or maybe it was Theories of Personality. One of those upper-level Psych courses. Still, even apart they had continued exchanging texts until almost midnight. The last text Robert had received from Patrick read, "Love you, sweetie. I'll see you tomorrow."

Then tomorrow had come and there had been no word. Robert had rolled out of bed at about half past ten Sunday, expecting to already have a text waiting from his boyfriend. Patrick usually sent a message after his morning jog, but there had been nothing. Odd, but at first Robert had not been alarmed. He'd sent his own good morning text, and had then taken a shower. After scarfing down a breakfast of cold Pop-Tarts, he'd tried texting again. When that generated no reciprocal response, he'd called and gotten the voicemail.

As morning gave way to afternoon, Robert began to grow concerned. Since they'd started dating, he and Patrick never went a day without seeing one another, and when they weren't together, they kept up a steady stream of texts and posts on each other's social media accounts. This radio silence was unlike Patrick, and vaguely disturbing.

By dinner time, what was vague had become quite solid. He'd contacted some mutual acquaintances, but no one else had heard from Patrick either.

Robert considered pounding on the door again, but he knew it was useless. Either Patrick wasn't in, or he was choosing not to answer.

There is a third option. Something could have happened, and he's lying in there unconscious or worse.

Robert imagined himself delivering a swift kick that would crack the lock, but instead he turned and hurried down the hall. While the idea that something may have happened—ruptured appendix, aneurysm, slipped and hit his head on the side of his desk—terrified Robert, that wasn't what he believed in his heart.

What he believed was that Patrick had grown tired of the relationship and was breaking up with him by cutting off all contact. Ghosting, Robert had heard this technique called. Avoiding the big breakup scene by simply vanishing from the other person's life. Ignoring calls and texts and hoping that the other party got the message and eventually faded from your life like a movie specter dissipating in a gradual dissolve.

Pushing away from the door, Robert left the dorm, heading out into campus with no real direction in mind, just letting his feet lead him on a random path. The pathways were busy this morning, students walking singly, in pairs, sometimes in groups, chattering away about things as inconsequential as parties, part-time jobs, and exams. Robert kept his head down and spoke to no one, not even the few who said hello to him as he stalked past.

When he finally looked up, he wasn't surprised to find he was walking down the road that led beside the bookstore. The cascading fountain gurgled behind its pressed sheets of glass. As he rounded the corner, he stepped onto one of the small wooden decks that thrust out into the lake on this end.

Of course he had been heading to the lake, even if his conscious mind hadn't been aware of it. He and Patrick had picnicked by the lake several times, usually down by the clock tower, and while Robert had never joined his boyfriend on his morning jogs, he knew the runs around the lake were so important to Patrick as to border on ritual.

Robert began walking along the path toward the rose garden and the dining hall beyond that, the route he knew that Patrick always took. Joggers, power-walkers, bicyclists were out in force, making the loop around the lake. Men, women, older, younger, parents pushing children in strollers, even a couple on a tandem bike. This time Robert met the eyes of every person he passed, part of him hoping he'd find Patrick on the trail even though it was much later in the day than the man normally went jogging.

I know his schedule. He has Art Appreciation at 9. I could just hang out by the classroom, waiting for him to arrive.

Robert thought that sounded a bit too stalkerish, but the truth was he felt stalkerish. He'd heard of people being love sick before, but he'd always thought it a silly expression meant to explain away the behavior of people who had temporarily lost their minds.

Now he knew better.

Of course, he realized that almost everything pertaining to love had seemed silly to Robert before he'd met Patrick, because Robert had never been in love before Patrick. He'd had numerous dalliances and affairs, dated men for a few months here and there, but he'd never known this kind of emotional dependency. A year ago, if asked whether or not he believed in the concept of soulmates, he would have answered with a cynical laugh, but what he felt for Patrick was powerful and profound and elemental. It wasn't a result of chemical responses or pheromones; it was a force of nature as fierce as a hurricane.

And as potentially destructive.

Robert certainly felt like he'd been through a hurricane, the damage leaving him in an emotional state of emergency. Love had lifted him to heights he had never suspected before, but now he saw that such a meteoric rise came with a price. Namely the possibility of plunging back to the ground without a parachute.

Just past the amphitheater, he turned to cross the bridge that spanned the tail end of the lake to avoid climbing the steep hill. Even walking at a leisurely pace along a relatively flat path, Robert found himself winded and sweaty.

Is that why Patrick dumped me? Because I'm so out of shape?

Patrick had never seemed particularly bothered by Robert's extra pounds, but then it was an unfortunate fact of life that what didn't bother people in the beginning could grow to bother them a great deal over time.

He chastised himself for being so weak. It wasn't like him. Normally he had a confidence that seemed almost disproportionate, which explained how he'd bedded so many men most would consider out of his league. A lot of that confidence was merely façade, an overcompensation to make up for not being the most enticing physical specimen on the market, but now the façade was slipping, leaving behind the self-conscious, insecure boy he'd been growing up.

As Robert passed a group of guys playing Frisbee golf to his right, he tried to grasp hold to the edges of his fleeing confidence, to force the mask back in place. If he was going to get dumped, he wasn't going to go out without a fight. Damn it, at the very least Patrick owned him an explanation and one delivered in person.

Pulling out his cell, he dialed Patrick's number again, leaving yet another message, this one less whiny and more firm. "I'm not just going to disappear, Patrick. If you think I'll just slink away into the night, you need to give up that dream. Whatever the hell is going on with you, I'm going to keep pestering and needling until you tell me. *Face to face.* So just suck it up, grow a sack, be a man, and call me back!"

As soon as he disconnected the call, Robert felt a wave of regret wash through him. Had he been too harsh? What if something truly were wrong? What if one of Patrick's parents had died and he'd had to rush home to West Virginia?

If something like that had happened, he'd have let you know. He wouldn't just leave you hanging.

Then again, when people were grieving, they weren't always thinking straight.

His mind also revisited the image of Patrick lying unconscious in his room. Such a scenario wasn't entirely out of the realm of possibility, and since Patrick didn't have a roommate, who would know?

As Robert started through the parking lot back toward the bookstore, he pondered whether he should call the police. Seemed a bit extreme, though as far as he knew no one had seen Patrick in the past twenty-four hours. On those police procedural shows his mother liked to watch, that was the rule. A person had to be missing twenty-four hours for the police to do anything.

Still, he hesitated. How foolish would he look if he called the police because his boyfriend was trying to ghost him? Talk about humiliation piled atop humiliation.

You'll feel a lot more than foolish if something really is wrong and you don't call someone.

Robert stopped halfway across the parking lot, near a dark stain on the pavement that he failed to notice, and pulled his cell phone from his pocket once again. Chewing on his bottom lip, he scrolled through his contacts until he found the number for Patrick's parents.

Taking a shaky breath, he selected the number and pressed SEND.

CHAPTER SEVEN:
BREAKING THROUGH

CLARE CROUCHED IN the far corner and clasped her hands over her ears as the pounding started on the wall.

"Please stop!" she screamed.

The pounding ceased, and Patrick's soft voice drifted to her ears. "Clare, honey, just calm down."

"You're going to get us into so much trouble when Big Daddy gets back."

"He may *never* come back, for all we know."

Clare pushed herself up and crossed to the plaster wall, putting her hands against it as if to form a connection with the young man she only knew as a disembodied voice. "Just hear me out, okay? Let me make my case."

"What, were you on the debate team or something?" Patrick asked with a laugh.

Clare ignored the question, though truth was that she had been on the debate team in school. Albeit very briefly. She found she wasn't cut out for it. She loved the idea of debate, a point-counterpoint exchange of opposing ideas with the intent of enlightening and informing. Unfortunately, what she'd discovered was that most did not share this definition. The other students on the team, as well as the faculty advisors, viewed debate as nothing more than loosely organized argument. Raised voices, insults, grandstanding—these traits were favored over logical thinking and respectful discourse. Clare had quit after Mr. Sharples yelled at her in front of the entire team and told her she lacked the requisite killer-instinct for debate.

"Just listen to me for a minute," she said. "There are only two possible outcomes here. Either he is going to come back, or he isn't. So let's evaluate the ramifications of those two possibilities. If he does come back and finds that you've beaten your way through the wall into my cell, he is going to punish us. More than likely severely. However, if he doesn't ever come back, what will really be accomplished by this? We'll both still be trapped, no closer to freedom. So, when you think about it rationally, the risk far outweighs any potential reward. It's not worth it."

Patrick was silent for a moment, and Clare hoped he was taking her words to heart. He dashed those hopes when he finally spoke. "One thing would be accomplished? You could have your fill of water from my spigot."

Clare closed her eyes and let out a shuddering breath. His blow hit below the belt. Her mouth was so dry, and her tongue felt like a sponge that had been left out on the windowsill in the sun for days until it became a hard brittle pad. She tried to work up some saliva but managed only a thin, sticky film. She swallowed and winced, her throat almost burning. The idea of cool water filling her mouth and sliding down her esophagus sent shivers throughout her body. She imagined herself diving into a clear pool and ducking her head under, taking deep gulping draughts, drinking until she became bloated with it, transformed with it. Her legs merging and scaling over, morphing into a mermaid sustained and enlivened by the water.

She opened her eyes from the dream into her harsh, barren reality. A great weakness overcame her, right down to the marrow of her bones and her very soul, sapping her energy so that she slumped back to the floor. "What does it matter?" she said miserably. "Even if you break through and I can drink, it will only be delaying the inevitable if he never comes back. Man can't live by water alone. Woman either."

"We have to *try*, Clare. What's the alternative? Giving up?"

"There's a certain comfort in giving up," she mumbled, not sure if he could hear her.

"No giving up," Patrick said with a vehemence that bordered on anger. "As long as we're alive, there's still hope. We can't give up."

"We'll see if you're still saying that when you've been here as long as I have."

"You've got to hold on, Clare. If you don't, you'll end up like Linda."

Thinking about the woman, about all she'd suffered and the madness that resulted, stung like a fishhook embedded in Clare's heart. She thought perhaps it would be best if Big Daddy stayed away forever, and Clare could just curl up on the floor and slowly wither away, breaking down to dust and rags.

"Clare, I listened to you, now it's your turn to listen to me," Patrick said, his tone soft and soothing. He did have a beautiful voice, and Clare couldn't help but wonder what the face looked like that went with that voice. She imagined a strong, dimpled jaw, chiseled cheekbones, piercing blue eyes, and thick, wavy hair. "You told me that having to sit helpless while you heard what was happening to Linda was extremely painful for you, right? Well, that's how I feel, knowing you're over there thirsty. Only maybe there is something I can do about that. You have to let me try to help. If not for yourself then for me."

Clare had to admit that his rationale was sound, but her fear was so great that it eclipsed all reason. A superstitious part of her believed that if Patrick didn't beat a hole through the wall then Big Daddy would never return; however, if Patrick did beat a hole through the wall then Big Daddy was guaranteed to return, as if the very act would summon him.

And he would be angry, and she dreaded to think what tortures he'd devise to discipline them.

As if sensing her thoughts, Patrick said, "I promise that if he does come back, I'll take full responsibility for this. I'll make sure he knows that you had nothing to do with it, and in fact begged me not to do it. If there is any punishment to be doled out, I'll take it all on myself."

Clare sighed. Cute and chivalrous, quite a combination. Of course, she reminded herself that she didn't *know* if he was cute. He may look nothing like the image she had built in her head; he could be fat and pimply for all she knew. Not that it mattered what he looked like, but she would be lying if she didn't admit she was curious.

If he did break through the wall, she could satisfy that curiosity.

She thumped her forehead with her palm, feeling her sanity sliding along a slippery floor. One minute she was thinking about how much she wanted to die, the next pondering if the guy imprisoned in the next cell was attractive. She found her thoughts becoming more and more unfocused, her moods fluctuating from apathy to despair to inappropriate giddiness at times.

"No giving up," she said under her breath then repeated the three words like a mantra. It wasn't much to hold on to, but it was something.

"What did you say, Clare? I didn't hear you."

She noted how Patrick kept saying her name, and she recognized this as a subtle attempt to ground her, to stop her sanity from sliding any further. She didn't know if it would work at this point, but she appreciated the effort.

"Go ahead," she said, crawling along the floor back to the far corner. "Get through the wall if you can."

The pounding started again immediately, the sound reverberating around the inside of her skull like a mad bird beating against the bars of its cage. She pulled her knees up to her chest and ducked her head, placing her hands over her ears once more. This muffled the pounding, making it sound almost like some kind of tribal drumming. Or at least what she knew tribal drumming to sound like on Nick at Nite reruns of that ridiculous old show *Gilligan's Island*.

The natives are restless, she thought and giggled. That inappropriate giddiness again.

She stole a peek at the plaster wall and could actually see it shaking with the force of each blow. An early childhood memory came back to her suddenly, something she had forgotten she ever knew. At five she'd been playing hide-and-seek with her father and somehow managed to lock herself in the hall closet. On the other side of the door, her father had become desperate, beating on the door and shouting for her to reach up and turn the latch on the doorknob. Clare had huddled at the back of the closet, more frightened by her father's ferocity than being trapped in the small, confined space. When he'd finally managed to kick the door open, she'd screamed and burst into tears even as he scooped her up and tried to soothe her.

She imagined her father on the other side of the wall, urgently trying to free her. There had been so much tension in her family since she started dating Hank, at times Clare felt like she hated her parents. Her father especially, who treated Hank with such contempt and intolerance. Yet at this moment she'd give anything to see his face, to feel his arms around her, lifting her up and whispering into her ear that she was safe, that the big bad monster couldn't hurt her anymore.

She heard a cracking and her head snapped up. The plaster wall had cracks in it now, cracks that bulged toward her with the next blow, white chalky dust raining down on the floor. Clare found herself thinking of those *Alien* movies where the helmet-headed creatures burst right out of people's chests.

As the first chunk of plaster fell out and hit the floor, she reached up to smooth her hair and tuck stringy strands behind her hands. She realized how ridiculous this was, trying to make herself presentable like a girl waiting for her prom date to show up at the door. She didn't need a mirror to know that she was an irredeemable mess. She hadn't bathed in months, and her skin felt grimy and sticky, her hair matted and tangled. She still wore the pink hoodie, jeans, and sneakers that she'd worn to meet Hank at Greer City Park the night she was taken, and at this point they were stained and ripped and hung loosely on her as she had lost quite a bit of weight. She had long become inured to the stench from the bucket she used as a toilet, but now she could smell it anew. It hadn't been emptied in days, half filled with urine and her watery stool. Of course, she realized some of the stink in the room came from her own unwashed body. What she wouldn't have given for a stick of deodorant or a bottle of perfume.

She knew it was silly to be worried about things like how she looked and smelled when they were in such dire circumstances, but apparently personal vanity was impossible to kill.

Another blow and more chunks of plaster crumbled in an avalanche, creating a window through which she got her first glimpse outside her prison for the first time since she'd awakened here. Suddenly a face appeared, not the romance novel Adonis she'd imagined but a clear-faced young man with dark eyes and full lips.

"Um, hi," Patrick said absurdly, as if greeting someone in a coffee shop. Their eyes locked, and then they both broke into a brief bout of laughter. Not the brittle, edge-of-madness giggling she'd done before this, but genuine laughter. It felt good; it felt cleansing.

"Fancy meeting you here," Clare said in her own attempt at humor.

Patrick examined the edges of the hole he'd made in the wall. "I'm going to widen this and then you can come get some water, okay?"

Clare nodded.

Patrick resumed beating on the wall with one of his buckets, also kicking at the plaster, until he'd made an opening almost as tall as him and the approximate width of a door. He stepped through and let the dented bucket clang to the floor with the sound of a gong. He wiped his right hand on his pants and held it out to her, like a proper gentleman.

She shook it and smiled shyly.

"Come on," he said, "let's go get you something to drink."

She followed him back to the hole in the wall. She could see that the wall consisted of two separate sheets of plaster sheetrock, set about five or so inches apart. Patrick had beaten through both sheets. As she stepped through the opening, she saw in the space between the sheetrock vertical two-by-fours placed at irregular intervals.

On the other side, in Patrick's cell, a pile of dogfood sat off to the side of the opening. He'd obviously emptied his food bucket to use it as a crude tool to break through the barrier between them. She scanned the room, finding it very much like her own except the door was different and there was a spigot along the back wall.

Clare wanted to keep her cool, but at the sight of the spigot, she let out a low moan and bolted over to it, dropping to her knees and twisting the valve. She stuck her entire head under the spray and gulped the water down, allowing it to soothe the burning sensation in her throat, moistening her chapped lips.

"Slow down," Patrick said, squatting next to her and placing a hand lightly on her shoulder. "If you drink too much too fast, you might get sick."

He was right. She could feel her stomach roiling and she pulled back, shutting off the flow of water and willing herself not to throw up. She sat on the wet floor with her legs tucked under her, eyes closed as she took several deep breaths until the storm in her gut passed.

"Sorry, I don't think I realized how thirsty I really was," she said when she felt certain she wasn't going to spew all over herself.

He gave her shoulder a squeeze then removed his hand. "That's okay. What are neighbors for?"

She laughed again, and then an embarrassing belch bubbled up out of her mouth, leaving a burning trail up her throat and a sour taste in her mouth. She could feel the heat of a crimson blush suffusing her face. "Excuse me."

Patrick smiled at her. "Don't worry about it. It's good to finally meet you properly, face-to-face and all."

"Too bad it couldn't be under better circumstances."

He didn't respond to that, just stared down at his hands dangling between his knees. "Do you mind if I go back into your room and check things out?"

"See if we can tunnel our way through the wall to freedom, you mean?" she said.

"Something like that. Sounds silly, I know."

"No, it's worth a shot. I'll help."

Patrick stood up first, before he took Clare's hand and helped her to her feet. His lips suddenly bowed downward in a frown, and his eyes filled with concern. "Are you . . . I mean, are you sure you're okay?"

At first she didn't know what he was talking about, but his gaze kept casting down her body then away. She looked down at herself and realized he'd noticed that the crotch of her jeans was blotched by a dark stain. The embarrassment she'd felt at the belch was nothing compared to the crippling shame that almost drove her back to her knees.

"I'm fine," she said, her voice too sharp, as if she were angry. Embarrassment often came out as anger, she mused. "It's just . . . well, since I've been here I haven't exactly had access to, you know, sanitary napkins."

She could read the confusion in Patrick's expression, and she also saw the light dawning as understanding hit. A blush crept into his cheeks and he looked away from her. "Oh," was all he said.

Clare was glad. This wasn't a subject she really wanted to discuss with a stranger. Or anyone, for that matter. Her own mother never even talked to her about menstruation, not really. When Clare was twelve, her mother had given her a book entitled *My Period and Me* and that had been that. She'd had the idea instilled in her that it wasn't merely a biological function, but something secret and shameful. In school, she sometimes encountered girls who talked freely about being "on the rag" and it made her vaguely sick to her stomach. Like hearing someone talk about their bowel movements or throwing up.

She'd gotten her period less than two weeks after being abducted. She hadn't dared mention it to Big Daddy. She had actually stripped from the waist down, wadded her underwear and tried to use it like a pad. It hadn't worked very well, saturating the cotton quickly and thus the stain that darkened her crotch.

She hadn't had to worry about it since, not having a real flow since that first time. Some spotting, bloody urine, but nothing like her regular period. She knew she wasn't pregnant; she and Hank had done some over-the-clothes groping but things had progressed no further. They had talked about it, and a part of her wanted to go all the way, to do the things the older girls said they'd done with their boyfriends. And they may have done it the night they were supposed to meet up at the park.

Only Big Daddy had gotten to her first.

No, she certainly couldn't be pregnant. She had read somewhere, possibly in *My Period and Me*, that extreme stress as well as malnourishment and dehydration could seriously throw a woman's cycle out of whack. She wished she could will her vagina closed altogether, leaving it smooth and rounded down there like a Barbie. Then she wouldn't have to worry about her period at all, or the fact that Big Daddy might do to her what he did to Linda.

Clare stepped past Patrick, who suddenly seemed very interested in his shoes, and back into the next cell. The young man followed her. "So what are we looking for?" she asked.

He walked over to the door and began running his hands along the wall to the left of it. "Loose stones, crumbling mortar, the feel of air slipping between the stones. Anything like that."

Clare, feeling energized now that she had sated her thirst, went to the back wall and began checking the stones. She worked silently and with total concentration. Although the odds still seemed greatly stacked against them, she felt a blossom of hope beginning to bloom in her chest. For the first time since her first days in this cell, she began to entertain the notion that she might actually get out of here, that she might return to her old life.

Of course, she could never truly go back to the life she'd led before Big Daddy had snatched her from the park. Her time here had profoundly changed her, on almost a cellular level. No, she'd never be the girl she was before, but she could build something new. She could find a way to put this ordeal behind her.

If they could find a way out.

When she'd made it halfway down the length of the wall, she said, "No luck here, how about you?"

When Patrick didn't respond, she turned and found that he wasn't checking the stones but was standing in front of the door, so still that she could almost believe he'd been frozen in place like a petrified tree. His head was cocked to the side, and his expression a study of single-minded focus, as if he were working out a particularly difficult math problem.

Stepping up to his side, she reached out and placed her fingers lightly on his back. He jumped and let out a startled shout then laughed at his own foolishness. "Sorry, I got a little lost in my head. Kind of forgot you were there for a minute."

Clare studied the door, trying to ascertain what about it had captured Patrick's attention. She failed to see the fascination. It was just a plain old door. "What are you thinking?" she asked.

Patrick stepped closer to the door, rapping his knuckles on the wood and grabbing the knob and rattling it. "This door isn't like the one in my cell."

Clare waited for him to continue, and when he didn't, seeming to retreat back into his own thoughts, she prompted him with a verbal nudge. "What does that mean?"

"Well, this was obviously once one long room and the plaster wall was added later. It looks like this door was also added later. Look, you can see where the stones were cut to make the opening to install the frame."

"Okay. What's the point?"

"The point is, this door isn't as thick as the one in my cell, and not being original to the room, it doesn't seem as firmly set in the frame."

Clare felt excitement building inside her, like the carbonation in a shaken soda. "Are you saying we may be able to get out?"

Patrick didn't answer for a moment, rubbing at his chin. When he did speak, he did so slowly, as if weighing each word before allowing it to leave his lips. "I'm saying that this door just may be the room's Achilles' heel. If there is a way out, this has got to be it."

CHAPTER EIGHT:
THE HAND OFF

GREG ARRIVED AT the hospital for his shift at 6:40 p.m. After stopping by the nurse's station to clock in and say hello to Janice, the Charge Nurse on duty, he headed to the break room to stow his lunch in the fridge and pour himself a cup of coffee from the pot in the corner. Lukewarm, but better than nothing. At least it was free for the nursing staff. He had a seat at the round table and settled for a moment, mentally preparing for another twelve hour shift, his fourth in a row. All he had to do was make it through one more night then he'd have the next three off.

Shelia, the dayshift RN that Greg would be relieving, stuck her head in the door. "Hey Greg-arious," she said, using the nickname she'd given him on his first day because he was so friendly. "Ready for Report?"

Greg nodded then finished off the coffee before tossing the cup in the wastebasket. Report was what all the nurses called the shift hand-off, where the outgoing nurse gave the incoming nurse all the pertinent information about the patients on the floor.

He grabbed the Report forms and followed Shelia out into the hall.

There were three patients on the floor this evening, one bed empty. They would go from room to room, as Sheila went over each patient's vitals, medications, new orders from the doctor. The same routine as every night. Patients may come and go, medications tried and adjusted, but nothing ever really changed.

Greg had become an RN at Pelham Medical Center just after graduating the nursing program at Greenville Technical College a year ago, but he'd been a CNA at Pelham for a full year before that. He knew the hospital as well as his own house. Maybe better. He certainly felt that he spent more time here than at home. He had sacrificed much—social life, sleep, holidays—for this job.

And was it worth it? He asked himself that question often. He'd gone into nursing after years of being a fitness instructor for a local gym because he had a deep desire to help others, to be of service to those who were ill. He had learned from his fellow classmates at Greenville Tech that not everyone pursued a nursing degree for that reason. It seemed more common people sought the job because it paid well and was a career path that offered stability. There was always a need for nurses. This seemed to lead to a lot of nurses with no real sense of compassion or empathy, nurses who treated patients like nuisances, the paycheck at the end of the week their only goal, their only concern. Certainly not the lives placed in their hands. Those were as inconsequential as dandelion fluff, something to be wiped off on pant legs or blown away into the wind.

This knowledge served only to reinforce Greg's conviction that a man like himself was desperately needed in the profession. Someone who appreciated the paycheck but saw it more as a bonus to the real compensation, which was the satisfaction at the end of the day that he'd made a difference in a patient's life. The feeling that he'd helped ease someone's pain, either physically or spiritually. He had to admit, some days he dragged himself home feeling like he hadn't accomplished much of anything, but other days he would get a smile or a thank you from a patient, or a gift from a patient's family for his kindness, and it filled him with a sense of purpose and conviction.

Still, the hospital life was hard. The twelve hour shifts, the all-nighters, the weekends and holidays, the required on-call days that often cut down on his time off and made it difficult to make plans. Not to mention the co-workers who didn't take the job as seriously as he did and therefore actually made the job harder.

Recently, Greg had applied for an RN position at a local doctor's office. He figured such a position would come with its own stressors, but it had to be better than the hospital. At least, he hoped. Of course, there was no guarantee he'd even get an interview for the job. In the nursing community, a position in a doctor's office was considered quite the cushy gig and was therefore in high demand. He'd be competing with probably a dozen or more applicants, some with considerably more experience than him.

"Earth to Greg," Shelia said, snapping her fingers in front of his face. "Are you even listening?"

Greg blinked and shook his head, embarrassed by

this lapse of professionalism. "Sorry, got lost in my own head for a minute. What were you saying?"

She looked at him with a cocked head and lips scrunched up to one side in a smirk. Greg found himself suddenly inexplicably angry. He had worked with Sheila a few times when she'd filled in for another night shift nurse, and he knew firsthand that she was often late for her shift, took breaks that exceeded the allotted times, and he knew at least once she'd been reprimanded by "getting an attitude" with a patient. What right did she have to look at him as if he were bad at his job?

You're being unfair, Greg. You don't know what Sheila's life is like. You're frustrated with work and taking that frustration out on other people.

He believed in the truth of this, but still he found it difficult to hold his tongue.

"I was saying," Sheila finally continued, "that Dr. Bice increased Gloria's Donepezil from 10mg to 15mg."

Greg jotted this down on his Report form then glanced down at the bed. Gloria Richardson was eighty years old, a widow the last thirty, and suffered from mild dementia brought on by the early stages of Alzheimer's. Currently she slept, seeming so small and delicate under the sheet, her hair pure white and so thin that it seemed not to grow out of her scalp but to coat it like spider webs. He mused that she appeared almost like a ragdoll that had been tossed in the wash and come out shriveled and shrunken. Last week she'd gotten confused when alone in the house, trying to climb up to the attic to find her wedding dress for reasons she had been unable to verbalize when brought in. She'd ended up falling off the ladder and breaking her hip and cracking her left tibia.

"I should also warn you," Sheila said then glanced down at the sleeping woman. She pointed toward the door with her chin, and once she and Greg were back out in the hall, she continued in a hushed voice. "Beth has gone out to dinner, but she'll be back and she's been in rare form today."

Greg groaned and rubbed at his temples as if a headache were forming. A headache the size of a five foot, two hundred-and-fifty pound woman with the screeching voice of a harpy.

Beth Richardson was Gloria's forty-five year old daughter. A rude, vicious woman who had rarely left the hospital since her mother had been admitted, and apparently considered it her life's mission to make the lives of all the doctors and nurses on the unit miserable. She complained about *everything*! The food her mother was served—half of which Greg suspected Beth ate herself—the lumpy pillows on her mother's bed, the fact that the TV bolted to the wall in the room didn't pick up enough channels. Most of all, she complained about the nursing staff. It seemed she thought the nurse assigned to her mother should be a private nurse, who only had to serve Gloria's—and by extension, Beth's—needs. She simply refused to understand that the nurse had other patients that required care as well.

She seemed to hold a particular antipathy toward Greg. He could do nothing right, in her eyes at least. She'd even lodged a formal complaint against him for being forty-five minutes late with his mother's medication one night, not realizing that the nurse could administer medications any time the hour prior or the hour following the actual med time. He wasn't sure why he seemed to draw so much of her ire, but based on the cross she wore around her neck and the Bible verses she constantly spouted, some of which she mangled, others he thought she made up entirely, he suspected it was because he was gay.

You're being unfair again. You don't know that is the reason; you're judging her based on her religion alone which is just as wrong as someone judging you based on who you love. Besides, you know there are ulterior reasons why she's so nasty to everyone.

True. Greg would have to say guilt was making Beth overcompensate and lash out. She had left her mother alone for only fifteen minutes to run down to the corner market and do some much-needed grocery shopping. She'd thought Gloria was sleeping, but in that brief quarter-of-an-hour window, the woman got up, pulled down the folding ladder to the attic, and plummeted her way to the hospital.

No doubt Beth felt responsible, and instead of dealing with that, she turned it outward, her guilt manifesting as a hyper-vigilance that resulted in hell for all the medical staff on the unit. Trying to alleviate her own feelings of culpability by criticizing the care given by others.

Of course, knowing this didn't lessen the dread of having to deal with her bitching for the next twelve hours.

Across the hall from Gloria Richardson was Mike Hardison, a forty-five year old father of two who had suffered a mild stroke. His recovery was nearly complete and he would likely be released in the next day or so. He was alert and in good spirits, his family present and eager to have him back home. His report went quickly and then they were on to the last patient.

Bernie Wilson.

Even though the man remained in a comatose state and had no family, hospital policy required that Report be given by the bedside of the patient. Greg understood the reasoning of that. Studies suggested that coma patients had at least some awareness of their surroundings, able upon waking to recount conversations held in the room while they were unconscious. One of the reasons why Greg made sure to speak to Bernie throughout his shift, as opposed to treating him like a piece of furniture.

"Not much change with Sleeping Beauty here, I'm afraid," Shelia said. When she saw Greg's shocked expression, she quickly added, "Sorry, sorry, bad joke. No change in his medication or his vitals. Dr. Bice says there has been some reduction in the brain's swelling but it's too early to say whether or not he will come out of the coma. I last turned him about an hour ago, and that was also the last time he was cleaned."

Greg nodded, silently grateful the man had been cleaned so recently. What not a lot of people thought about regarding coma patients was that their bodies did not stop eliminating waste just because they were unconscious. It fell to the nurses to change and clean them. Adult diapers made it more manageable but it was still far from pleasant.

"And that about sums it up, unless you have questions about anything," Sheila said, so obviously eager to leave that her body was practically vibrating. Not that Greg blamed her. He was much the same way at the end of his shift.

"I got it. Go on home and get some rest."

"Are you kidding? I'm off tomorrow. I'm going out on the town tonight."

"Don't get too wild. I don't want to have to treat you because you got so drunk you fell off your porch."

"That only happened once, and there were special circumstances. It was my birthday."

The two shared a laughed, and then Shelia headed out. Greg lingered in the room for a moment, looking down at Bernie. Sleeping Beauty, indeed. The man had been struck by a car the day before, and he had yet to regain consciousness. Perhaps he never would. Greg didn't like to think that way, but he knew it was possible. Sometimes people never recovered from comas; that was simply a fact of life.

Yet that was hard to believe just looking at Bernie. He wasn't wasted or sallow of complexion. Quite the contrary. He was robust with good color. Greg recognized the thought as trite and cliché, but he could in fact almost believe Bernie merely slept. He'd wake eight hours from now, rested and refreshed and wondering why he had a PICC line stuck into his left arm, supplying him with fluids, meds, and nutrition.

Greg knew that looks could be deceiving. Often people incubating virulent diseases went months, sometimes years, without even realizing it. Then again, he also knew that sometimes those whose prognosis was bleak made unexpected recoveries that could only be described as miraculous. Greg considered himself a man of science, but he also had a deep respect for the mysterious, things that science could not adequately explain. He didn't necessarily think in terms of the supernatural. After all, many things now elucidated by science were once considered supernatural in origin; once even natural elements like rain and fire were viewed with superstitious fear. But he believed the smartest people acknowledged what they didn't know.

If Greg had a philosophy, it was simply this: where there's life, there's hope. And often hope fueled life. He'd seen people cling to life through sheer force of will, and conversely he'd seen people die less from their ailments than from simply giving up. Therefore, Greg thought his greatest job was to feed his patients a steady diet of hope.

"Hey Bernie, how you doing tonight?" Greg said softly, laying a hand on the man's shoulder. He liked to think if Bernie were aware, then hearing a friendly voice and feeling a reassuring touch would be healing.

If he heard or felt, Bernie gave no indication, lying in continued silence.

The room was bare. No flowers, no balloons, no Get Well cards. No family or friends. The air even felt stagnant, lending to the atmosphere of despondency. Greg mused there was nothing sadder than a patient who never received visitors. Greg tried to make up for it, to be not just a caregiver but a friend.

"I'm going to take good care of you," Greg said. "You're going to get through this, I believe that. You'll wake up and be home before you know it. Back home where you belong."

Greg turned away from the bed then and didn't see the fingers of Bernie's right hand twitching or the sudden fluttering of his eyelids.

CHAPTER NINE:
CLARE'S ABDUCTION

CLARE PAUSED AT *the open window, one leg thrown over the sill. She held her breath for thirty seconds, listening intensely for any sound, however small, that her parents might be up. The house silent, the only sounds the whirring whisper of the heat pump and the trip-hammering of Clare's own heart. She'd waited until nearly midnight to head out, and her parents were always in bed by ten. Surely they'd be fast asleep by now, dreaming of a life in which they had a perfect daughter that never disappointed them. Much as she sometimes dreamed of a life in which she had parents who didn't treat her like a total idiot.*

Once she was satisfied her father hadn't gotten up for a midnight snack or her mother to use the restroom, Clare ducked through the window and dropped the foot to the ground below. Reaching up, she slid the window shut most of the way, leaving a tiny gap at the bottom to ensure she wouldn't have any trouble reopening it when she returned home.

She didn't want to go around the front of the house because that would require she pass by her parent's bedroom window, so instead she went through the backyard, through the gate in the fence, and into the alley that ran behind all the houses on the block. There were no lights here, and she walked down the alley as if through an underground tunnel, the shapes of the houses dark, almost shapeless silhouettes against the darker night. The night was cool, and she found herself wishing she'd worn a thicker jacket. However, when she'd dressed, her mind had been geared more toward cuteness than practicality.

Still, she was warmed by the thrill of rebellion, doing that which she was not supposed to be doing. A mere year ago, she'd have scoffed at the idea of her sneaking out of the house through her bedroom window like some cliché from a teen angst movie. She'd never thought of herself as a bad girl.

And she still didn't. She wasn't one of those girls in school who sneaked smokes in the restroom and cut class and sometimes dropped out after their stomachs started to bulge. Clare consistently made the A/B honor roll, brushed and flossed after every meal, cleaned her room without being asked. So, why did her parents treat her like the bad seed?

Because she had fallen in love. They could dress it up any way they wanted, but that was the long and short of it. She'd fallen in love with a boy of whom they didn't approve. Hank also made honor roll almost every semester, was exceedingly polite and thoughtful, had never had any scrapes with the law, not even a speeding ticket. So, why were they so determined that she not see him anymore?

Because his parents were Muslims. No other reason. As if they thought he carried a bomb around *in his backpack and might blow up the school one day. It was ridiculous. I mean, if a guy claimed God told him to drive his car into a crowd, her parents didn't hold that against all Christians. She tried to make that very point to them, but they wouldn't hear it. They simply forbade her from dating Hank and then grounded her when she called them ignorant bigots.*

They couldn't stop her from seeing him at school, sitting with him at lunch, meeting at his locker after class. They had taken her cellphone and tablet as part of her grounding, and while she needed her laptop for schoolwork, she was only permitted to use it in the living room or kitchen where they could monitor her to ensure she didn't IM or email Hank.

Which meant they had to get creative. At lunch today, he'd asked her to meet him at Greer City Park at half past midnight. She had agreed without hesitation, despite the fact that she lived two miles from the park.

As she walked down Pennsylvania Avenue, passing the public library on her right and the post office on her left, she took in the silence of the night. No cars passed her on the street, the buildings and nearby houses were dark. She heard a dog barking in the distance, the slush of tires back behind her somewhere, probably on Wade Hampton Boulevard, but these sounds only served to accentuate the deep stillness and quiet that closed over the town like a glass dome.

Greer was far from a metropolis, a relatively small city of approximately twenty-nine-thousand citizens, but Clare had never seen it this deserted before. She imagined herself in one of those old black-and-white *Twilight Zone* show that she watched a marathon of last New Year's, a woman alone in an abandoned world.

Yet she wasn't scared. She figured she should be, a young girl walking by herself at midnight on empty streets. She lived in a dangerous world; even a place like Greer had its share of murder, rape, robbery. Just last month a guy strangled his wife before shooting himself in the head just down the road in Taylors, which was an even smaller town than Greer.

So why wasn't she afraid? In fact, she felt enclosed in a bubble, as if nothing could touch her and no harm could come to her. Her skin tingled with anticipation, and a sense of invulnerability wrapped around her like a warm blanket. She was on her way to see the man she loved; she felt this protected her like the witch's kiss on Dorothy's forehead in The Wonderful Wizard of Oz. And much like Dorothy's journey down the yellow brick road, while the path may seem full of danger, her safety was assured.

With a laugh, she silently chastised herself for such silly, childish thoughts. This wasn't like when she was a little girl and would fantasize about a prince riding up on a white horse and rescuing her from a tower to take her back to his castle to be his princess. Hank was real; her feelings for him were real. This wasn't a storybook romance, but love in all its painful and splendid glory.

The road narrowed and passed through a neighborhood of shabby homes built so close together she figured a person in one house could reach through a window and hold hands with a person doing the *same next door. She picked up her pace, not out of fear but because it was nearly fifteen after twelve and she still had a way to go before she reached the park. She should have left the house earlier, but she had wanted to be sure her parents were asleep before making her break. She didn't want to get to the park too late and risk Hank arriving, waiting, then leaving, thinking that she'd stood him up.*

As she walked, her mind drifted to thoughts of her parents. She hated them right now, their closed-mindedness and their irrational prejudices. She hated them but also hated herself a little for hating them. Until she'd started dating Hank, she had gotten along fairly well with her parents. Not perfectly, there had been fights and anger, but never anything serious. Their treatment of Hank had revealed a side to her parents she had not known existed, hadn't even suspected.

And the disillusionment hurt. She supposed it was all a part of growing up, realizing your parents were flawed and weren't always right about everything. Knowing that this experience was normal, and most young people went through it, didn't make it any easier. She felt she'd lost something indefinable but important, and as a result a hollowness now existed at the center of her being.

As she turned left onto Main Street, headed for the downtown area, she shook her head to rid herself of such distressing thoughts. She focused her mind not on her parents but on Hank. A shining example of the goodness that still existed in the world. His love for her would fill the hollowness. He had a way of keeping her centered and grounded, helped her see herself as less of the gawky, awkward kid she'd always felt she was and more like a confident, self-assured woman.

As she made her way down Main Street, a car approached coming in the opposite direction. She tensed, ducking her head down. She feared the car might stop and the driver ask what she was doing out so late. What if it was someone who knew her parents? Not likely, but also not impossible.

The car passed without slowing and she breathed a sigh of relief. A block and a half ahead, the police station loomed on the left side of the street. Clare did not want to walk by it, not at this hour. She veered right onto Victoria Street. She knew this would take her across Trade before intersecting with Poinsett right at the park's entrance.

The closer she came to her destination, the more the excitement thrummed through her, coursing through her veins and rattling her bones before concentrating into a sweet ache between her thighs. The feeling was new to her, an ache she'd occasionally relieved in the bath.

When Hank had asked her to meet him at the park, he hadn't intimated anything that would suggest theirs was to be a carnal rendezvous, but in his eyes she'd seen the unspoken suggestion and she tried to reply with her own gaze that she understood and she was ready. If it turned out she were wrong and he didn't make a move, she might very well make one of her own. The detachable showerhead might do in a pinch, but what she truly wanted was Hank. The time had come to make her fantasies of his naked body pressed against hers a reality.

Of course, there was the question of where they would do it. Neither of them had a car, and she doubted even pooling their money would come to enough for a motel room. That only left the park. She'd heard some of those loose girls in the locker room saying they'd done it in the park. On one of the benches, on top of a picnic table, in the gazebo down by the pond, one girl even said she and her boyfriend had done it on the slide down at the children's playground. However, the consensus seemed to be that the safest location for a late-night hookup was the small graveyard just off the park. If you did it behind one of the larger monuments, even if a cop did patrol the area, he likely wouldn't venture into the cemetery.

As she crossed over Trade Street, her footsteps quickened until she was practically jogging. The time was 12:35, but she could see the entrance up ahead, the sign that arched over the paved path into the park. She dashed across Poinsett without even checking for traffic and ran down the path to the round, brick fountain where she and Hank were supposed to meet.

She found herself alone. She made a complete circle around the fountain, calling Hank's name in a stage whisper. The fountain was lit from within, casting a wavering light up through the water. Small jets sent curving sprays into the air, making the whole thing look like a magical birthday cake.

The fountain sat right next to the open-air amphitheater, and she stepped to the edge of the cement stage, squinting out at the seating tiers, the scant moonlight unable to penetrate much of the darkness of the area. "Hank," she said in a hiss. "Are you out there?"

No response.

That anticipatory ache had turned to a queasiness. She had been less than ten minutes late; surely Hank would have waited longer than that before leaving. Maybe he'd wandered down to the far end of the park by the pond and the Canon Center. She considered going that way herself but figured it would be best to stay at the designated meeting spot. If he had wandered off when she wasn't here at 12:30 on the dot, surely he'd make his way back shortly.

Or maybe he changed his mind and decided not to come. Maybe he decided you were too much trouble and he'd be better off with some girl he didn't have to sneak around to see.

This thought elicited a pained groan from Clare. She didn't want to think of herself as one of those silly, melodramatic girls who lived for her boyfriend; she considered herself more independent than that. She had to admit she did depend on Hank. Not as her sole source of happiness or anything so ridiculous, but as someone who understood her in a way that no other human being ever had. Someone who accepted her exactly as she was, flaws and all, and didn't make judgements. She'd never had that level of unconditional acceptance before, not even from her parents, and now that she'd gotten a taste for it, she did feel a sense of mourning at the prospect of losing it.

"Stop it," she said to herself. She'd gotten to the park late because she'd wanted to make absolute sure her parents were asleep before sneaking out; chances

were something similar had happened to Hank. He would be here. She knew it.

Taking a seat on the rim of the fountain, she stuffed her hands in the shallow pockets of her hoodie. That pleasant ache returned, a moist heat that made her squirm on the cold bricks. She wasn't without fear. She'd heard that the first time could be painful and there would more than likely be a little bleeding. She didn't like pain and she loathed blood. Changing her pad during her own period often made her gag. Still, she did not doubt it would be worth it to be that close to Hank, to feel him on top of her, inside her. That would bond them in a way that her parents could never break.

Patting her pants pocket, she confirmed that she had the condom packet. Last year during Sex Ed, the instructor had handed out condoms after giving a demonstration on how to use them on a cucumber. Some parents had protested the class, not allowing their kids to take it, but Clare's folks had thought it was a great idea. Much like her mother giving her the copy of My Period and Me, *her parents loved it when someone else would teach their daughter the complicated lessons of growing up.*

Clare had squirreled the little foil packet away in her sock drawer, and there it had stayed for the last year. When the instructor, a butch-type gym teacher with a square jaw and a bob haircut, had placed the condom in Clare's hand, she hadn't been able to imagine a time when she might actually use it. Perhaps that wasn't entirely true, otherwise why hadn't she simply thrown it away? Maybe even then she'd known that this moment would come.

She found herself suddenly wondering how long condoms were good, if they had an expiration date or something. She hadn't thought to check. She loved Hank, but she certainly didn't want to end up pregnant at fifteen and become some afterschool special cliché.

She perked up at the sound of footsteps approaching from the other side of the fountain. She couldn't see who it was from here, the second tier of the fountain blocking her view, but who else could it be besides Hank?

Feeling giddy and uncharacteristically playful, she decided it would be fun to scare him. Slipping off the rim, she crouched down and began to crab-walk around the fountain, trying to move as stealthily as possible. The footsteps began to circle around in the opposite direction so Clare paused, clamping a hand over her mouth to stifle the giggles that wanted to escape.

As the footsteps drew closer, she tensed then leapt up, yelling "Boo!" The man who was not Hank let out a high-pitched squeal and stumbled back a step. At least she assumed from the build that this was a man, dressed in black jeans and a black sweatshirt, as if wanting to blend with the shadows of the night. His face, his entire head actually, was concealed by a ski-mask that only revealed his eyes and mouth.

Clare was too stunned to be scared, at least at first. She had been so prepared to see Hank that it took her mind a moment to adjust to the fact that this wasn't him. She was more perplexed than frightened, at least until the man raised his arm and she realized he gripped a baseball bat. Even then, the fear was distant, what she felt watching a horror movie.

When the masked man recovered from his own surprise and took a resolute step back toward her, Clare's fear coalesced and became more urgent. She turned and began to run, sucking in air in preparation for a scream. Before so much as a squeak left her lips, she felt an explosion in the back of her head and went tumbling forward, striking her chin on the pavement, her teeth snapping on her tongue, her mouth filing with blood.

She could feel the man behind and over her, but she did not turn her head to meet his eyes. Instead she scanned the park, and she realized she was looking for Hank, desperately believing he would come to her rescue. Her prince on a white horse, after all.

This is the real world, Clare! There are no princes, no knights, no heroes! No one is coming to save you! You have to save yourself!

She began to claw at the pavement, pulling herself forward, trying to scream. She seemed to have no breath in her lungs, and the pain in her head was so large that she feared she was going to vomit. As she dragged herself along the pavement, she could hear the clop of the man's shoes as he followed her. She also heard a soft, oily laugh. The bastard was enjoying himself.

She couldn't believe this was happening. It was like something out of a movie, not something that occurred in real life. Most people who were attacked were attacked by people they knew, not by a stranger in a mask who toyed with them and delighted in their suffering. That was the stuff of celluloid nightmares.

"Help me," she tried to shout, but it came out as a croak and the effort made it feel as if the back of her skull were caving in.

The stranger walked around her until she was staring at a pair of mud-encrusted work boots. She started to cry, hating her weakness, wishing she could be one of those bad-ass chicks from comic book movies or fantasy TV shows. Instead, she only groveled there at her attacker's feet, sobbing out pleas.

She glanced up the length of his body just in time to see him swinging the bat toward her again.

And then she knew nothing for a while.

CHAPTER TEN:
NIGHTMARES

PATRICK JOGS AROUND the lake just before dawn. The campus is utterly deserted, and no lights shine from any of the buildings. No sound interrupts the utter stillness; even his shoes slapping the pavement are silent. He notes with no real surprise that the clock tower by the lake has been replaced by a missile, long and phallic, smoke churning up from the bottom as it prepares to be launched. Distantly he can even hear a robotic voice commencing a countdown. *10 . . . 9 . . . 8 . . . 7 . . . 6 . . .*

As the path rises up into the wooded area at the far end of the lake, he slows his pace, lips twisting down into a frown. The trees seem to crowd closer together than he remembered, and they are larger. Monstrous in fact, thick and stretching to the heavens like redwoods. Knots and whirls in the bark look like grimacing faces. The branches reach out for him like sharp-tipped claws, scratching at his exposed skin, drawing blood and covering his body with the dull sting of papercuts. The pavement beneath his feet becomes cracked and broken, resembling ice floes in an arctic sea. Thin, sinewy weeds as tall as his knees sprout up from the cracks, sliding around his legs like snakes, impeding his progress. The trees on either side seem to lean forward over the path, meeting above him and blocking out any light from the stars or rising sun. The darkness is total, and yet he still can see. As if he is part mole with vision attuned to the night.

Now he slows to a walk as the pavement completely crumbles away and he finds himself traveling a tiny slice of a dirt trail through the woods. He continues to climb a steep slope even though he feels by now the path should have curved around and started on a downward trajectory. A light snow sprinkles down from above like powdered sugar, dusting the earth.

Up ahead, the trail dead-ends at a snarled deadfall of snapped branches, most of them as big around as a man and twice the length. The deadfall rises at least twenty feet into the air and he stands before it, wondering if he should attempt to climb over. If the whole thing collapses while he is at the top, he could get seriously injured.

From behind him, he hears a low growl. At first he thinks it must be the rumble of the missile taking off, rocketing into the sky to hone in on its distant target. Yet he can still hear the countdown, though now the numbers are going up. *11 . . . 12 . . . 13 . . . 14 . . . 15.* As the growl increases in pitch and reverberates on the air, he can tell this is an animal sound, something wild and ferocious. Not a wolf or a bear or even a prehistoric dinosaur, but some beast that is the amalgamation of all these things. The most lethal traits of every creature that ever crawled the earth distilled into one entity.

An entity that now stalks Patrick.

He turns slowly, looking back the way he came. He sees nothing, but the growling continues, somewhere to his left. The creature is hidden by the trees, visible only as a deep shadow that moves in the small gaps. A gargantuan shadow almost as tall as the trees themselves.

With the cracking sound of bones breaking, the trees begin to part, one of them snapping near the base and falling across the path and knocking down another on the other side. From the newly made gap in the tree line the creature steps into view. It seems to be made from the very trees itself. Large with spindly, splintering limbs, multi-jointed and numerous like a giant, wooden spider. The fat center of its body seems made of gnarled, bent branches and prickly leaves, leaves that looked hard and glossy, forming a kind of armor. Though Patrick can detect no mouth, the thing roared with the sound of exploding suns and toppling mountains and dying gods, making the very ground beneath Patrick's feet quake.

Fear floods through him like ice water in his veins, and he turns and begins scrambling up the deadfall. Bark flakes off like dead skin, branches cracking and buckling beneath his feet. Thin shards of wood, like toothpicks, dig into his hands, and branches snapped to the wicked points of spears slash at his face as he fights his way toward the top of the pile.

Behind him, he can hear the creature's legs skittering closer. Glancing over his shoulder, Patrick screams as he sees one of the thick limbs descending toward him. He rolls quickly to the right, narrowly avoiding being crushed, but the thing's limb crashes through the deadfall, and Patrick feels the unstable collection of branches beneath him give way. Suddenly he is falling, tumbling through the air and ricocheting off shattered branches like a pinball. He feels a few of his ribs break, and the shard of a branch stabs deep into the thigh of his left leg.

After falling for what felt an eternity, he hits the ground on his right side and pain flares as his shoulder dislocates with a loud *pop*! He is pelted with falling debris as the entire deadfall caves in on top of him, entombing him.

He tries to scream again, but no sound escapes his lips. The weight on top of him crushes him into the dirt, pulverizing bones and piercing flesh. He struggles against it, trying to claw his way out, attempting to dig himself out of the rubble and back into fresh air . . .

Patrick jolted awake, his body drenched with sweat. For a moment he could still feel the weight on the deadfall grinding down on him, but then he realized that had only been a dream, a particularly vivid nightmare. He was safe.

Only, as he looked around at his surroundings, he realized that wasn't true. He'd waken from one nightmare into another. Next to him, Clare slept curled up in a fetal position, snoring softly, her thumb in her mouth like an infant.

Patrick pushed himself up so that he sat with his back against the wall, and he groaned and clutched his stomach as a cramp seized him. Biting his lip to keep from crying out, not wanting to wake Clare, he braced himself against the wall and got to his feet, a hand still to his stomach as he stumbled through the hole in the plaster wall into the other cell. He slid his pants down to his knees and crouched over the bucket in the corner, hoping Clare wouldn't wake up and find him in this position.

What came out of him was watery and hot, as if lava poured from him. The smell twisted his stomach, the stench of sickness and rot. When his business was done, he slid his pants back up, wishing he had something with which to wipe, but such creature comforts were little more than the whiff of a dream. He crawled away from the bucket, not wanting to look inside at his own mess, and huddled in the corner, hugging his knees to his chest. The nightmare had a residual grip on him and was not easily shaken off. He still felt as if he were suffocating, being crushed, and closing his eyes he could vividly conjure up the image of the giant creature made from the woods themselves. He shivered then clutched his stomach as more cramps tore through his abdomen.

These pains did not indicate he had to go to the bathroom again; these were hunger pains. So intense that for a moment it felt as if someone was scooping out his insides with a rusty spoon. He leaned forward and planted his head on his knees, breathing slowly and deeply, until the pain subsided somewhat. It didn't go away, but it became more manageable.

He scooted himself over until he could reach the spigot. Turning the valve, he drank deep but the lukewarm water cascading down his throat did nothing to sate the hunger that gnawed at him. He imagined a nest of squirming rats in his belly, eating their way toward freedom.

Damn it, you're stronger than this. It has only been a couple of days, at most. Power through this.

Even if your body has to subsist on its own fat stores for a while, so be it. It's too early for you to be thinking what you're thinking.

Patrick realized he was staring off toward the pile of dog food he'd dumped out of the second bucket before using it to batter his way through the plaster wall, and his mouth was watering. He slapped himself lightly on the cheek and muttered, "Get a grip, man!" He couldn't afford to let panic seize control of him. Not now, not when it was so important that he keep his wits about him.

Mind over matter. He was hungry, yes, but he wasn't starving. It was too soon for that. He had to push such thoughts from his mind so he could focus on the problem of getting out of this hell. Not only was his own freedom on the line but Clare's was as well. Clearly, she teetered on the precipice of giving up, so it was imperative that he remain strong.

No giving up.

He got to his feet, refusing to use the wall for support this time. He crossed the room resolutely, repeating his mantra in his head. *No giving up, no giving up, no giving up . . .*

As he stepped through the hole in the plaster, he discovered that Clare was awake, sitting cross-legged in front of her food bucket, scraping out a handful of kibble and tossing it in her mouth. When she saw Patrick standing there, she smiled, chewed, swallowed, then held out another handful. "Want some breakfast?"

The sight of her there, chowing down on dog food, was certainly not appetizing, but it worried Patrick that he also didn't find it utterly repugnant either.

"Today's the day we're getting out of here," he said, his voice too loud. "What do you say?"

Clare's expression became pinched and squirrely. When he'd first broached the subject of possibly getting out of here, she had seemed excited; now she appeared to be reverting back to a state of fear. People often talked about the fight-or-flight response to dangerous situations, but most didn't realize there were three possible reactions. Fight-flight-or-freeze. Clare definitely seemed to be gravitating toward the freeze option.

"We're trapped in here," she said. "I don't think we should waste our energy trying to escape from a room that is inescapable."

Patrick walked to the door, stood in front of it and studied the frame intensely, as if he could stare a hole right through it. "I told you, I don't think the room is inescapable. The door is the weak link."

"The door is locked, you already tried it. And we both tried breaking it open and it didn't work."

That was true. Patrick and Clare had spent half an hour launching themselves at the door, hoping to bust the lock. Though the door was not as sturdy as the one in Patrick's cell, they had been unsuccessful. He couldn't verify that Clare had been giving it her all, but Patrick certainly had. He'd continued beating at the door for ten minutes after Clare called it quits and lay down on the floor. Disappointed, he'd eventually curled up next to her and fallen asleep.

However, he wasn't going to throw in the towel so easily. It simply wasn't in his nature.

Ostensibly talking to Clare but really thinking aloud, he repeated some of the things he had noticed about the door earlier. "The pins for the hinges are on the outside, as well as the screws for the doorknob. That definitely doesn't work in our favor. The door itself isn't an exact fit for the frame, there's a little bit of space all the way around. I think I can see some kind of slide lock or deadbolt."

"You're right," Clare said. "Whenever Big Daddy comes or goes, I hear him sliding the lock."

Patrick nodded then grabbed the doorknob and rattled it. "This knob is cheap. I should be able to knock it off no problem."

"Knock it off?"

Patrick turned back to the girl and said, "Once the lock got stuck on my closet door. No matter what I just couldn't get the door open. And like here, the pins and the screws were on the other side. Every bit of clothing I owned, including all my shoes, were in the closet. I had to get in."

"So, what did you do?"

"Took a hammer and wacked away at the doorknob until it broke off."

"We don't have a hammer."

"No, but we have that," Patrick said, pointing toward the dented bucket he'd used to beat through the plaster wall. "If I can get the doorknob off, that will take care of that lock. Of course, that still leaves the deadbolt."

"What can we do about that?" Clare said, getting to her feet. Patrick was glad to see her more engaged again, the fear in her warring with hope. He needed to continue to fan that spark.

"I've got some ideas about the deadbolt," he said, which wasn't entirely the truth. Still, he wanted to keep her hopeful. "But first things first. Let's work on the doorknob."

CHAPTER ELEVEN:
SUSPICION

SHERIFF HAMMETT LOOKED up at the knock at his office door. One of the newer deputies, Sanchez, stuck his head in. The man looked vaguely ill and a little nervous. "Um, Chief?"

Hammett forced himself not to roll his eyes. He hated the moniker "Chief." It made him feel like he was one of the Village People. Still, it was what most of his officers called him and he had come to tolerate it, if not accept it. "What is it, Sanchez?"

After a slight hesitation, Sanchez said, "They're back."

Now Hammett did roll his eyes. He didn't even have to ask who *they* were. Over the past few months, there had become only one *they* referred to in the office. *They* are holding on line one. *They* have been blasting the sheriff's department on Facebook. *They* published another Letter to the Editor in the *Greenville News* accusing the police of ignoring leads. *They* have sent twelve emails in four hours.

They are here. Again.

Mr. and Mrs. Barrett.

"Should I tell them you're busy interrogating someone or . . . something?"

Hammett sighed. He was temped, sorely tempted, but he shook his head. "Just send them in."

"You sure, Chief? You know they're going to heap more abuse on your head."

"I know. Send them in."

"You're the boss," Sanchez said then ducked back out.

Hammett took a moment to straighten the items on his desktop, composing and bracing himself. He knew he should refuse to see the couple. Sure, then they would alert the local news media and tell them that he refused, making him out to be the bad guy, but after talking to them they would still alert the local news media and tell them he was being insensitive to their concerns. A classic damned-if-you-do-damned-if-you-don't scenario.

So why see them when they would trash him regardless? Simple. He felt sorry for them. They were a couple grieving for their daughter. True, they didn't know that Clare was actually dead, but with each day that passed, that possibility seemed more and more likely. Hammett had a daughter of his own, three years younger than the Barrett's girl, and he could only imagine the turmoil with which they must be living. In some ways, he mused it might actually be better if they had definitive proof Clare was dead. The uncertainty, the not knowing, left them in a Schrodinger's cat limbo that could only serve to exacerbate the pain.

For that reason alone he would talk to them, he would let them rant and rave, he would let them blame him. It wouldn't get them any closer to having their daughter back, but it would give them a direction toward which to turn their helplessness and anger and fear. It was the least he could do for them, since he didn't seem able to locate their daughter.

Phil Barrett came in first, his posture rigid and his brow furrowed so that his eyebrows came together like two kissing caterpillars. Sue Barrett followed, her back bent as she slumped over, her mouth trembling. This was how they always appeared, he a furious exclamation point and she a tremulous question mark. They sat in the two chairs in front of Hammett's desk.

"Would you like some water or coffee?" Hammett asked.

Ignoring the question, Mr. Barrett leaned forward with his elbows planted on his knees and said, "We found a lady who lives on Cannon Street who says she saw a dark-complected young man entering the park on the night Clare disappeared."

Hammett maintained steady eye contact and kept his expression neutral, not wanting the couple to think he wasn't taking their concerns seriously. "Let me guess, Brenda Hoffman?"

Mr. Barrett sat back with a reluctant nod. "Yes, that's right."

"We've already spoken with Ms. Hoffman, on more than one occasion. The dark-complected young man in question she saw only from behind with a group of four or five other youths, and they entered the park at approximately 7 p.m., more than five and a half hours before your daughter was abducted."

Mr. Barrett slammed his palms down on the top of Hammett's desk, causing his penholder to topple over, spilling out a variety of writing utensils. He then stood and began to pace around the office, his body shaking with frenetic energy. "Why won't you take us seriously? I'm telling you, I know in my gut that damn Bukhari kid is responsible."

Hammett took a few breaths before responding, but he could feel his temper flaring like a match. They simply wouldn't stop hounding poor Hank Bukhari, and he knew they had used the prevailing prejudice in the country to turn a lot of the community against the Bukhari family as well. Officers had responded to a call only two nights ago of people throwing rocks at the family's home, and someone had slashed the tires of Dr. Bukhari's car outside his office. The family was being treated as vicious criminals, despite the fact that Dr. Bukhari had been practicing medicine in Greer for almost twenty years and his wife was a second grade school teacher at Crestview Elementary. Seeing how quickly the town had turned on them put Hammett in mind of "The Monsters are Due on Maple Avenue." It was a little scary.

"We've been over this a dozen times already," Hammett said in a weary tone. "Hank Bukhari has an alibi. He has admitted he was supposed to meet your daughter at the park that night, but his parents caught him trying to sneak out of the house, and they were up for two hours lecturing him on responsibility and honesty."

"And you take their word for it?" Mrs. Barrett said, pulling a tissue from her purse and swiping it under her leaking eyes. "Of course they would cover for him. For all we know, they are in on it. None of those people can be trusted."

"Those people?" Hammett asked pointedly. "You mean . . . doctors and school teachers?"

Mr. Barrett strode to the desk and leaned over it. "You know exactly who we are talking about. Wake up, this country is at war. These fucking illegals are coming over here to infiltrate our country and take over. None of us are safe."

"You need to cut down on your FOX TV viewing. Dr. Bukhari and his wife have been U.S. citizens for almost twenty years now. They've been model citizens."

Mr. Barrett snorted derisively. "That's what they want you to think. It's called lulling you into a false sense of security."

Hammett felt his control beginning to fray. Their paranoid conspiracy theories were becoming wilder and more untethered from reality. A sign of the times, surely.

Truth was, Hammett had thoroughly investigated Hank Bukhari. The boyfriend who had arranged to meet the missing girl the very night she disappeared . . . of course he had been the prime suspect.

However, any good cop could tell you that the most obvious suspect isn't always the guilty party.

There was Hank's alibi, yes, but there was also the security footage from the park. Most of the lamp posts throughout the area were equipped with security cameras, and the footage from that night showed Clare's abduction from several different angles.

Her abductor wore black clothes and a ski mask that completely covered his head. He had been seen entering the park from the small side street that led between the cemetery and the amphitheater, then making his way around to the fountain where he'd hit her twice with a baseball bat then carried her unconscious form back the way he'd come. The theory was he'd probably parked on Cannon Street, probably at the Spinning Jenny concert hall. Unfortunately, there were no cameras outside the park.

Despite the man's face being concealed, his build was too large and too wide to belong to Hank Bukhari, and the perpetrator did not wear gloves, revealing the hands of a Caucasian male.

This evidence had done nothing to persuade Mr. and Mrs. Barrett. They argued the Barrett family could have hired someone to abduct Clare. Why? Their reasoning seemed to fall apart regarding possible motive. Of course, they seemed to think having brown skin and an accent was motive enough.

Hammett took a moment to try to see past the couple's anger and bitterness and bigotry to the humanity beneath. It wasn't easy, but Hammett took his job as public servant seriously and part of that job was recognizing the basic humanity of all the citizens of Greer. Keeping that in mind, he could see Mr. and Mrs. Barrett for what they truly were. Broken, despondent people, their hearts full of broken glass, looking for some way to alleviate the pain even if that meant spreading it around. Unpleasant, but understandable.

"Listen," he said softly, "if I thought for a second anyone in the Bukhari family was responsible for your daughter's abduction, I would be interrogating them every day. You have to believe that."

"Then why don't you?" Mrs. Barrett pleaded.

"Because you are barking up the wrong tree," Hammett said as patiently as he could. "I want to catch the sonofabitch who took your daughter, but I want to get the *right* guy."

Mr. Barrett wrapped his arms around himself, leaning slightly forward so that his posture began to mimic that of his wife. His face became a collection of tics and twitches, as if he were about to undergo a change, a metamorphosis. When he spoke, his voice was hushed and choked. "Hank Bukhari is the right guy."

Hammett stood and walked around his desk. He hesitated but then placed a hand lightly on Mr. Barrett's shoulder. He almost expected the man to jerk away, or even throw a punch, but instead he stood still and silent, allowing the contact.

"No, he's not," Hammett said. "I know in some ways that it would make things easier."

Mr. Barrett looked up at him with bloodshot eyes. "Nothing could possibly ever make this *easier*, not until my daughter is home safe and sound."

"Of course, I didn't mean . . . all I'm saying is that life isn't like an episode of *CSI*. The guilty party isn't always obvious, and he or she rarely leaves a trail of convenient clues that lead investigators right to them."

"And sometimes the guilty party is never brought to justice," Mrs. Barrett said. "Isn't that right?"

Hammett considered his response, but he figured even a well-meaning but empty lie would only be more hurtful in this case. "That's right, sometimes the guilty party is never caught."

Mr. Barrett took a deep breath and shook the sheriff's hand off. Hammett worried the man was about to explode again, but his voice was level and calm when he said, "So if you don't think it was the Bukhari kid, then who do you think it was? Do you have *any* leads?"

Hammett considered his words again, but this time out of shame. Out of his own sense of failure and inadequacy.

"We're working hard on the case," he said, recognizing the statement as an obvious dodge and realizing it would be obvious to the Barretts as well. "We don't have any solid leads at the moment, but we're not giving up."

He could see the disgust in Mr. Barrett's eyes, and Hammett knew that disgust was warranted. Truth was, there were no real leads. All they had was the security footage but that offered no clues as to the identity of the kidnapper. He had canvassed the surrounding neighbors but could find no potential witnesses that might have seen a strange car near the park at half past midnight that morning. And unfortunately the city of Greer had never shelled out the cash necessary to install traffic cameras at the lights. Therefore, once the mysterious man in black carried Clare Barrett out of range of the park cameras, the girl effectively disappeared. All Hammett could hope for was that someone would come forward with information that would jostle the investigation out of this holding pattern. Maybe someone saw a girl fitting Clare's description in a car at a gas station. Grasping at straws, Hammett realized, but the average citizen would be surprised to learn how often cases got solved just that way.

It was either that or wait until a body was discovered.

"What about the FBI?" Mrs. Barrett asked, her eyes continuing to leak. Hammett didn't think he'd seen the woman since her daughter's disappearance that she hadn't been crying. He wondered how she had any moisture left in her body. "Why isn't the FBI involved?"

"The FBI only gets involved if a kidnapping involves the abductee being transported across state lines, and there is no evidence of that here. We have been coordinating our efforts with the state police, as you know. Everything that can be done is being done, I assure you."

That just isn't very much at this point, he didn't add.

For a few minutes, no one in the room spoke, the silence building up like rising water, inching toward their faces to drown them all. Finally Mr. Barrett turned to his wife and said, "Let's get out of here. As usual, there's no one here that wants to help us."

Hammett started to respond but realized it would do no good, so he stood silently and watched the couple leave. What could he say to them? He wanted to help them, but he didn't have the means to help them.

He walked back to his desk and dropped into the seat, as exhausted as if he'd done an hour of cardio. His meetings with the Barrett's always left him drained and vaguely depressed, but he knew that was nothing compared to what they felt. In a weird way, he considered it his penance for not being able to do more for them.

"Everything okay, Chief?" Sanchez asked, stepping into the office. "We all going to be fired?"

Hammett sputtered a laugh. "Sometimes I think I wouldn't mind that so much."

"I didn't hear as much screaming this time around."

"Yeah, they're beginning to accept that there's not much we can do at this point, which is actually pretty tragic. I think I prefer their anger to their resignation."

Sanchez offered a sympathetic nod then turned to leave.

"Hold on a sec," Hammett said. "While you're here, where do things stand with Neil Baker?"

"He's paid his fines in full. I really see no reason not to reinstate his license."

"What about the guy he hit?"

"Still in a coma. If there's any change, the hospital should call us."

Hammett thought it over a moment then said, "Go ahead and get the ball rolling with Baker's license."

"Will do, Chief." Sanchez started from the office but paused in the doorway.

"Anything else? Hammett asked.

"No, or . . . well, maybe. Just wanted to tell you I heard there may have been another disappearance."

"Here in Greer?"

"No. Greenville, out at Furman University. I have a friend who works security there. Apparently yesterday a student was reported missing by his boyfriend. There has still been no sign of him, and today his parents came down from somewhere up north and are raising a stink about it."

"Any reason to suspect this disappearance is related to Clare Barrett?"

"Not really," Sanchez admitted. "Just two young people, both gone missing in the same county. Thought you should know."

"Thanks. I'll call Sheriff Randolph in Greenville,

see what he has to say, and keep me posted if you hear anything more."

"Sure thing."

Once Hammett was alone, he logged onto his computer and pulled up the Barrett file again. He'd been over it dozens if not hundreds of times in the past couple of months, but he still held out hope that on a repeated viewing he might make some connection previously missed, a connection that would break the case wide open.

After all, grasping at straws was how many cases got solved.

CHAPTER TWELVE:
GETTING THROUGH THE DOOR

CLARE STOOD AGAINST the back wall, fingers plugging her ears, as Patrick used the already dented bucket to beat on the doorknob, denting the bucket even further. A dull, hollow *gong*! reverberated in the air with every strike.

The sound also seemed to reverberate in her bones, making her feel as if her skeletal frame was going to simply break apart and she'd collapse onto the floor, a collection of ivory shards in a loose sack of skin.

Of course, she realized this was only the fear talking. Fear that Big Daddy would return and discover what had been done, the hole in the plaster wall and the damaged doorknob, and he would make them suffer for their insolence and disobedience. She realized they'd really gone too far to turn back at this point. They couldn't repair the hole in the wall. Their best course of action was to continue forward and try to get out of this cell before Big Daddy got back.

Be brave, Clare, she told herself. *No giving up.*

Patrick beat on the doorknob from above, causing the knob to begin to bend downward. She heard the crack of the wood as it splintered around the knob. After several moments, Patrick paused, panting and wiping sweat from his forehead. He squatted down to inspect the knob, grabbing it and yanking at it.

"Thing's resilient," he said. "Don't worry, though, I'll get this fucker off."

Standing, he resumed pounding, this time bringing the bucket up underneath the knob, bending it back up to its original position then even higher. He came at it from first one side then the other. The wood continued to splinter, and Clare could tell the doorknob was becoming looser. Patrick kept up his barrage for almost fifteen minutes before finally collapsing to his knees, letting the bucket clang to the floor next to him. The thing was so dented and malformed that it almost resembled a soda can that had been crumpled and tossed in the trash.

Patrick planted his hands on his thighs, slumped forward and gasped for breath. Clare approached and knelt next to him. She wanted to reach out and touch him but didn't know if he would appreciate the gesture. He seemed lost in another world, as if he weren't even aware of her at his side.

Clare looked at the doorknob. It too was dented and bent . . . but not dangling. He was right, the thing was resilient and could take a beating.

Finally she reached out and placed a hand on his shoulder. He flinched at first but then settled, letting her hand stay there. "It's okay, Patrick. You did your best. It's okay."

That was what she said, but it wasn't what she felt. She felt things were far from okay. All this had been for nothing, breaking through the wall and battering the doorknob. They were still trapped here, and eventually Big Daddy would return and he would hurt them. He would hurt them bad. Tears welled in her eyes.

"I'm not done," Patrick said as his breathing evened out. "Just resting, getting a second wind."

With her free hand, Clare reached out and touched the damaged bucket. The opening had folded in on itself to the point that it would never hold anything again. "I think you pretty much destroyed this. What are you going to do? Use mine?"

Instead of answering, Patrick pushed up to his feet and turned back to the door. This time he attacked the knob with his bare hands, wrenching it one way then the other, up and down. He did this without making a sound, which made it somehow more frightening. The wood around the knob cracked even further, chunks of it breaking off entirely and falling to the floor like a rain of splinters.

She wanted to tell him to stop, but all she could do was watch him, mesmerized by his ferocity and his silent rage. After a few minutes he focused his energy on pulling the knob as far to the left as he could, chords standing out in his neck as he put all his strength into it, then forcing it all the way to the right. He did this repeatedly, the motions forceful and quick, almost like he was rowing. More wood fell away, widening a hole around the knob.

After several more minutes, as he wrenched the knob back to the left he suddenly fell over, landing hard on his back. Clare cried out and hurried to him, worried he may have busted his head on the cement. At first, she thought he was weeping, but she realized with puzzled shock that he was laughing. She couldn't understand what could be so funny, at least not until he held up his hands.

He still gripped the doorknob. Both of them actually, the dented knob that had been on the inside of the room and the pristine knob that had been on the outside of the room, still connected by the spindle, the latch that slid into the jam to lock it protruding from the midway point. She glanced back at the door and saw a hole a little smaller than a baseball where the knob had been, the wood around it broken.

"I did it," he said triumphantly, holding the doorknobs up like a trophy he'd won. "I motherfucking, bet-your-ass *did it*!"

Clare realized she was laughing as well, and she gazed at the knobs as if at a holy relic, one with magical powers that had to be viewed with reverence and respect.

"What now?" she asked.

The question seemed to cut through the hysteria that had gripped Patrick, and he sat up, setting the knobs aside. With an expression of renewed determination, he hurried back to the door, hunkering down and staring through the hole.

"What do you see?" Clare asked, coming up behind him, hands clasped to her chest.

"Not much. It's dark in there, which suggests there are no windows in the rest of the basement either. I think I can make out the stairs just across from the door."

"Can we get out? I mean, now that you've removed the doorknobs, does this mean we can get out?"

"Well, there's still the deadbolt to contend with,"

Patrick said, straightening up. He shoved his shoulder into the door again. Clare joined him. The door seemed not quite as secure in the frame as before, but still solid enough that it seemed obvious they weren't going to bust through this way.

Patrick stepped back and examined the door with a thoughtful, far-away expression, unconsciously stroking his neck with the fingers of one hand. In his eyes, Clare could see him trying to ferret out a solution to this problem.

She took a turn staring through the hole into the dark basement. She'd seen glimpses of this area when Big Daddy would come in to bring her food or change a bucket, and it had taken on mythic proportions in her mind. As if this was a doorway to a fantastical world like Oz or Wonderland or Narnia. A world of adventure and freedom and beauty. If she could only get through the doorway. She stuck two fingers through the hole, as if just touching the air on the other side might be the key to her escape.

"I've got an idea," Patrick said behind her, his voice firm and sure. When she glanced back, he was striding back to the plaster wall, grabbing the edge of the hole and tearing chunks away.

"What are you doing?" Clare asked.

"I want to get to one of those two-by-fours, use it as a battering ram."

That taste of freedom promised by that small round window onto the world on the other side of the cell acted as a powerful motivator, and Clare helped him widen the hole until they revealed one of the vertical two-by-fours. It was actually a series of three two-by-fours crudely nailed together end to end to reach from the floor to the ceiling.

Patrick asked her to stand back and then he proceeded to kick the beam until he finally knocked the top of it lose. With his hands, he wrestled it the rest of the way out, a couple of long rusty nails raining down on the floor. Nails also protruded from either end. He brandished the thing like a club.

"Think you'll be able to bash the door open with that?" Clare asked as he stalked back across the cell.

"Probably not, but I might be able to widen this hole."

Patrick began beating the end of the beam against the door right where the knob had been. Slivers of wood flew through the air like little missiles. His teeth were gritted in a skull's smile, and a ferocious, primal scream erupted from his throat, so loud and gravely that Clare feared he would snap his vocal chords.

She could see the wood around the hole where the knob had been beginning to stave inward, and this seemed to invigorate Patrick and he attacked with renewed vigor. Clare noticed drops of blood hitting the floor and realized Patrick's hands were bleeding; he was probably getting his share of splinters in his palms from the two-by-four, but he did not let this deter him.

Clare wasn't sure how long he beat at the door. Time seemed to lose all coherence, becoming more an abstract concept than a firm law, as she watched in a state not unlike a trance. There was something primal about Patrick's ferocity, making him seem to her like some ancient warrior, maybe an Aztec. She felt a rush of warmth spread over her skin. In that eternal moment, she loved him. Not a sexual or even romantic love. He was beautiful, the way an angel was beautiful. A strong, ferocious avenging angel.

On his next thrust of the two-by-four, the beam punched through the door. Patrick stumbled and fell, losing his grip. He landed on his back, but the beam remained suspended in air, sticking out of the door like a diving board.

"Are you okay?" Clare asked, rushing to his side. She could see that his hands were indeed pierced by so many slivers of wood that they appeared like cacti.

Patrick sat up, shook his head, then stared at the two-by-four, a dawning light of excitement flaring in his eyes. Scrambling to his feet, he placed both hands against the end of the beam and started to push, his feet planted and his face going red with exertion. The two-by-four moved an inch, punching even further through the door.

"Help me," he said.

Not knowing exactly how to help, she got behind him, put her hands on his back, and pushed him while he pushed the two-by-four. Her feet kept slipping on the cement and she'd started to slide back. She braced both her forearms across the small of his back and moved her feet as she were running in place. They both grunted and strained and the beam ground through the small opening.

Slowly, at least until about the halfway point. Then a large fissure shape, like a lightning bolt ran up the door from the hole where the knob had been almost to the very top, and the beam began to slide through rapidly. Patrick went with it, but Clare lost her footing and fell to her knees.

The two-by-four went all the way through the

opening and she heard it clatter to the floor on the other side of the door. Patrick stood staring at the door, his eyes glossy and dazed.

"It worked," he said, and she could hear the disbelief in his voice. "It actually goddamn worked!"

Clare looked at the hole where the knob had been, now enlarged to roughly the size of a grapefruit. She didn't want to be the one to piss on the birthday cake, but she frowned at Patrick and said, "I don't see what good this does us. It's not like we can fit through that opening."

Patrick gave her a look as if she were a mentally deficient child who had just asked the color of Wednesday, then he scurried over to the door on his knees and began to slowly thread his arm through the hole.

Feeling foolish, Clare released a shaky laugh. "Oh, sorry, my brain isn't exactly working on all cylinders right now. Been under a little bit of stress lately."

Patrick ignored her weak attempt at humor, focused on getting his arm through the opening without cutting himself on any of the jagged pieces of wood. He got his arm through all the way to the shoulder, his eyes squinted in concentration and his tongue poking out between his teeth. He stayed that way for nearly a minute. Clare could hear his hand slapping on the other side of the door.

"Can't reach the lock?" she asked, the delicate bubble of hope that had formed in gut on the verge of bursting.

"I almost can," he said. "My fingertips are barely brushing it, but I can't get enough purchase to actually slide the bolt."

"I'd try, but my arms are shorter than yours so—" Clare stopped speaking abruptly, and she imagined a cartoon lightbulb shining above her head. "I've got it!" she exclaimed and ran back to the plaster wall. She scanned the floor then bent over and picked up the item she was looking for. She hurried back to Patrick and held the slightly bent nail out to Patrick. "Maybe this will give you the extra length you need."

Now Patrick looked at her as if she were the beautiful angel, and she felt herself blushing. He pulled his arm back through the hole, moving too quickly, and one of the sharp edges of wood dug a scratch from his elbow halfway to the wrist. He hissed air in through his teeth and clutched at his bleeding forearm.

"Shit," Clare said, wishing she had something to cover the wound with. She could use her hoodie as she had a T-shirt on underneath, but the thing was so filthy at this point, it likely wouldn't be very sanitary.

Patrick shook his head and waved it off. "Doesn't matter, I'll live. Give me the nail. You're a genius."

Her blush deepening, she handed him the nail.

Placing his arm back through the opening, he resumed his concentration and she could hear the minute *clink* of metal against metal. That bubble grew inside of her until she thought she might be swallowed up by it and carried away like that good witch in the *Oz* movie.

She heard a louder *clunk* then Patrick let out a whoop of triumph. With his arm still through the opening, he pushed against the door and it opened, Patrick allowing the momentum of the door to free his arm.

Clare felt herself swoon like some character in a

cheesy romance novel. She wondered if she might be dreaming or hallucinating. After all this time trapped here in her cell, the open door before her seemed unreal and frightening. It suddenly seemed safer to stay in the cell, the hell she knew.

Patrick seemed to suffer no such anxiety as he immediately stepped through the doorway into the gloom of the rest of the basement. Almost as if he were walking willingly into the mouth of a beast, unconcerned that he would be chewed and digested and shit out into the cosmic void.

Get a hold of yourself, Clare. This is your chance, this is freedom. Stop cowering like a baby and get out while you can!

Forcing her feet to move, she followed Patrick.

There were no lights outside the cell, only the dirty yellow illumination from the wire-covered bulb through the doorway bleeding into this larger area. The floor was cement and the walls stone with no windows, just as in the cells. No furniture that Clare could see except a scuffed wooden table shoved against the wall to the right, underneath which were a nearly empty bag of Alpo dog food and several small wedge-shaped yellow boxes. Inside Clare saw small green pellets and realized with a roiling of her stomach that she was looking at boxes of rat poison.

Somehow the idea that there were rodents down here where she'd been sleeping, that they could have been crawling around her while she slept, was even more horrifying than the imprisonment alone. A shiver caused her to spasm as if in the grips of a mild seizure as she imagined the fat furry creatures, the gray of dirty dishtowels, crawling over her slumbering body.

Patrick stood at the bottom of the stairs, looking up at the closed door. "Seems the only way out is up."

"Do you think that door is locked too?"

Patrick shrugged. "Only one way to find out."

He bounded up the stairs, and Clare trailed along behind him, actually grabbing hold of the back of his sweatshirt as if afraid she might lose him. At the top of the stairs, Patrick hesitated for a second, hand hovering above the knob. Clare flashed on a story she'd read for English back in middle school, the one about the two doors, one of which had a tiger behind it and the other a lady, and the guy had to choose like the world's worst game show. Only here was only one door, but their fates seemed to hang in the balance all the same and the tension was overwhelming.

"Here we go," Patrick whispered then grasped the knob, turning it easily. Clare expected the door to refuse to open, another deadbolt barring them from escape, but the door creaked open on rusty hinges.

The two stared at one another for several seconds then broke into giggles, like children who had sneaked down early on Christmas morning and peeked at their presents. Clasping hands, they walked out of the basement together.

Finding themselves in a short hallway. To their right was a wall and across from them an alcove containing a beat-up washer and dryer. To the left, the hall stretched a few feet before intersecting with another hall in a T-juncture. The floor was a dirty linoleum tile, the walls an off-white or possibly just white that had grown dingy over time.

"Okay," Patrick said, turning to her. "Let's find our way out of here and—"

His words cut off as a low, menacing growl filled the air. Turning toward the T-juncture, Clare gasped when she saw a black dog turn the corner. The thing was tall but lean, muscles flexing under its short fur, ears sticking straight up like on Batman's cowl and its teeth bared as the growling increased in pitch. A Doberman Pinscher, she thought, though she wasn't an expert on dogs, being more a cat person herself.

"Back in the basement," Patrick said, placing his hand on her shoulder and nudging her gently back through the door. "Don't make any sudden movements, just go real slowly."

As she began edging her way back into the stairwell, the dog stopped growling and began snarling and barking and rushed down the hall toward them, its nails scratching against the tile.

Patrick shoved her the rest of the way through the doorway and followed, slamming the door behind him. A heavy blow struck the door, making it rattle in its frame, and under the apocalyptic barks Clare could hear the thing clawing at the door, trying to dig its way through to get at them.

Clare clung to the railing as huge wracking sobs erupted from her. "What are we going to do now?" she wailed.

Patrick stared wide-eyed at her, but she saw no answer in that stare.

CHAPTER THIRTEEN:
DINNER TIME

PATRICK STOOD WITH his back against the door, watching as Clare bent over, weeping hysterically. *What are we going to do now?* she'd asked, but he had no response to that one. He could feel the vibrations in the wood as the Doberman launched itself at the door as if trying to use its head as a battering ram, much as Patrick had used the two-by-four as one on the cell door.

The two-by-four!

He dashed down the stairs, moving so suddenly and quickly that it startled a gasp out of Clare. At the bottom of the stairs, he snatched up the beam from where it had fallen once punching its way through the hole where the doorknob had once been. He held it near one end and gave it a few test swings, as if it were a baseball bat. The thing was lighter than he would have liked, lacking substantial heft, but it did have the wicked nails sticking out of either end.

"What do you plan to do with that?" Clare asked. She'd come down the stairs and taken a seat on the bottom step. She was no longer crying, instead looking like a discontent child pouting over not getting what she really wanted for her birthday.

Patrick swung the two-by-four a few more times. "I'm going to use it as a weapon, beat the dog's head in if I have to."

A derisive snort was Clare's only response.

"What? You have any better ideas?"

"No, but . . . "

"But what?"

"Just because I don't have any better ideas doesn't mean your idea is any less crappy. I mean, did you see that animal? He could snap that hunk of wood in two. Besides, the stairwell is so narrow, you're not really going to be able to swing your club at the dog when it comes barreling though the door."

Patrick felt anger rising toward Clare and her pessimistic attitude. He thought he preferred her whining or even the crying. Her desultory cynicism was too close to giving up, and he knew that kind of defeatism could be contagious.

After all, she was right. Though the Doberman was no longer barking or beating at the door, Patrick could still hear the animal growling and clawing at the wood. No doubt that if Patrick opened the door again, the dog would pounce in an instant, and there wasn't much room to maneuver on the stairs. His plan was a bad one.

And yet it was the *only* plan.

"I have to try," he said to Clare. "I can't sit down here waiting to see what fate some creep psycho has in store for me. I have to be proactive. I have to *do something!*"

Clare seemed unmoved. "And what about me? If

the dog gets past you—and let's face it, it probably will—then how am I supposed to defend myself? With stern words and a glare?"

"You want a weapon? I'll find you a weapon," Patrick said, his voice rising sharply to a shout. He was under enough stress without the girl turning into such a little snit. He realized he wasn't being entirely fair; she was, after all, under just as much stress and had been under it for longer. Yet knowing this did nothing to keep his temper in check.

He propped the two-by-four over his shoulder like a club and stalked back into the cell. "Come on," he yelled back over his shoulder. "Let's find you a weapon, goddamn it!"

First thing he spotted was the bucket he'd used to beat the doorknob, but it was a mangled mess so he kicked it aside, cursing at the resultant pain in his toe. He certainly wasn't going to touch either one of the shit buckets, which only left Clare's food bucket. He grabbed and upended it, sending what dog food remained raining down on the floor.

"What are you doing?" Clare shouted, knocking him out of the way and falling to her knees so suddenly that he was sure she must have hurt herself. She began to scoop the dog food into her hands. "This is all I have left to eat!"

"You're not seeing the bigger picture here. If we can get out of here, you can have a real meal instead of eating dog—"

Clare looked up at him, distracting from her scrambling by the abruptness with which he stopped speaking. "What is it?" she asked.

"An idea," Patrick said than lowered himself next

to her, placing the beam on the floor. "Put the dog food back in the bucket."

"What? Why?"

"Just do it, please."

She seemed skeptical, as if afraid he was going to steal it from her, but she did drop what was in her hands to clink at the bottom of the bucket. He then laid the bucket on its side and swept the rest of the food inside with his hand.

He hurried through the hole in the plaster wall into his cell, stopping at the pile of dog food from where he'd emptied his own bucket earlier. This he added to Clare's bucket, too. For his final stop, he went back out into the basement and poured what little remained in the Alpo bag into the bucket, filling it three-quarters full.

Clare watched him from the doorway of the cell. "I don't understand what you're doing. How does consolidating our food help?"

"It isn't for us," Patrick said, bending down to retrieve the three boxes of rat poison from beneath the table. He emptied the contents one by one into the bucket, then the bucket he shook it so that the green pellets mixed in with the dog food, as if he were tossing the various ingredients of a salad.

"Do you think that'll work?" Clare asked.

"Absolutely!"

Patrick sounded more confident than he actually was. He didn't know the exact reaction a dog would have eating rat poison, but he figured anything that would kill a human would surely kill a dog. And rat poison would kill a human . . . wouldn't it? Three boxes full would have to, he thought. Of course, he had no idea how long these boxes had been down here or if rat poison lost its potency after a while.

A lot of unknowns in this plan, but it was unquestionably better than trying to beat the Doberman to death with a stick.

"What if it won't eat the food?" Clare asked. A smidgen of hope had returned to her voice, but her questions retained their pessimistic nature.

"If the asshole who abducted us hasn't been around to feed us then he hasn't been around to feed his dog either."

"He could have one of those feeders that continuously fills the bowl as the dog eats."

Patrick had had about enough of these roadblocks the girl kept throwing up, particularly since they were all logical and things he should have thought of himself.

"A dog like that," he said, "is not going to turn down food. Trust me, he'll eat it."

"How are you going to get it to him?"

"Easy, open the door and toss the bucket out into the hall."

Patrick realized his mistake even as the words left his mouth. Clare's expression suggested she recognized it too. This plan had the same fallacy as his previous plan: as soon as the door was opened, the Doberman would bust through and attack. They had to somehow get the dog away from the door.

Scanning the basement area again, his gaze fell through the cell doorway and alighted on the two-by-four. Inspiration struck like a lightning bolt and he put the bucket down and grabbed the edge of the table, dragging it across the basement so that the legs scraped along the floor.

"What are you doing?" Clare said.

Instead of answering her question, Patrick gestured with his chin toward the cell. "Grab the two-by-four and follow me."

Much to his surprise and delight, Clare didn't question him further but did what she was told. He continued to drag the table, which was heavier than it looked, to the far wall and shoved it up against the stones. He glanced at the ceiling, again gauging it to be about twelve feet high. The table stood about four feet from the floor, he'd guess Clare to be around 5'5", and the two-by-four at least four feet. The math should work out.

"Okay," he said, turning to Clare. "I'm going to need your help to pull this off."

She stood with the beam planted beside her, holding it near the top, looking oddly like one of those old farmers from that painting with the pitchforks, *American Gothic*. "What do you need me to do?"

"Climb up on the table and beat on the ceiling with the two-by-four. Hopefully it will sound like a knocking somewhere in the house and—"

"And it'll lead the dog away from the door," Clare finished. "Not a bad idea."

"Thanks. Probably won't fool the thing for more than a minute, but long enough to toss out the bucket. Then if we're lucky, it'll gobble up the food and settle down for a nice endless nap."

With a nod, Clare scrambled up onto the table. She lifted the two-by-four until it touched the ceiling. "I think this might work."

"Me too," Patrick said, going back to retrieve the bucket. "Wait for me to give you the word then start beating against the ceiling like crazy. Really cause a ruckus."

"Aye, aye, Captain," she said with a smile that gave Patrick a brief glimpse of the carefree young woman she must have been before all this happened.

He crept up the steps, placing each step softly, trying to make as little noise as possible. At the top, he crouched on the landing, putting his ear to the door. The dog was no longer growling, but he could hear the animal's breath on the other side, and occasionally he would scratch at the wood. He could imagine the Doberman lying in front of the door, standing guard, biding its time. *Waiting.*

Turning his face away from the door and speaking in a stage whisper, he said, "Okay, Clare, *now*!"

She started up right away, pounding the two-by-four on the ceiling, a steady rapid staccato like machine gun fire. With his ear to the door, he heard the dog begin to growl and then to bark, but at first it did not leave its sentry post.

"Keep it up," he said, though he doubted Clare could hear him over the barking and the noise she herself was making. Nevertheless, she did keep it up, the jackhammer sound reverberating throughout the entire basement.

Finally Patrick heard what he'd hoped to hear, the click of the dog's nails on the tile and the barking moving away from the door and down the hall. With a steeling breath, he grasped the knob and opened the door wide enough to swing the bucket through the gap. It struck the washer before hitting the floor, the food and pellets spilling out. He didn't dare poke his head out, but he could hear the scrambling/scratching as the dog turned abruptly on the linoleum and the barking began to increase in pitch as the animal hurried back. He slammed the door quickly then once again felt the impact as the dog torpedoed into the wood. Patrick panted and gasped as if he'd done something physically taxing.

"Did it work?" Clare asked, equally breathless, as she ran up to the foot of the stairs, the two-by-four trailing behind her like some kind of bizarre security blanket.

Patrick held a finger to his lips and returned his ear to the door. The Doberman continuing snarling and scratching at the wood for several more moments, but then it seemed to back away, growling deep in its chest, then quieted as the sound of lapping and crunching reached Patrick's ears, a sound sweeter than a newborn baby's cry or hearing "I love you" whispered softly in the ear at the height of passion.

Clare abandoned the beam and climbed the steps. "Did it work?" she asked again.

Patrick let loose with a wild laugh. "I think so, I think it's eating. And sounds like the bastard is really scarfing it down. Must have been damn hungry!"

Clare sputtered a twittering laugh of her own and began to chew on her thumbnail. "So . . . what now? What do we do now?"

Placing his back against the door, Patrick allowed himself to slide down until he was sitting on the landing. "Nothing we can do but wait."

"For how long? How long will it take for the poison to . . . you know, *work*?"

Patrick looked up at Clare, who looked back at him with naked need. His adrenaline rush was fading fast, leaving him feeling exhausted, and he simply didn't have the energy to keep up the façade of in-control savior he'd been trying so hard to project. He threw his hands up in the air and said, "I don't know. I guess it'll take just as long as it takes."

Still chewing on her nail, Clare sat next to him and after a moment leaned her head against his shoulder. He placed an arm around her, not quite giving up the savior role, after all, and within moments they were both asleep.

CHAPTER FOURTEEN:

CONFRONTATION

ROBERT HAD JUST left Manly Hall a little after 8 a.m. when his cell phone rang. Glancing at the screen, he recognized Mrs. Young's number.

He answered immediately and said with desperate hope, "Any news?"

Silence from the other end then a sigh. "I guess that answers my question. I was calling to see if you had heard anything from Patrick."

"No, ma'am," Robert said, feeling near tears again. He'd been in a constant state of crying or just-about-to-cry for the past couple of days, leaving him feeling perpetually exhausted and dehydrated. "So I guess that means the police haven't come up with anything new?"

"No. Well, actually yes, but nothing that helps us. Nothing that tells us anything we didn't already know."

Robert meandered aimlessly past the library, heading toward the front of campus with no particular destination in mind, his feet moving on autopilot. "What do you mean?"

"They located a woman who was walking at the lake Sunday morning, and she said she was fairly certain he passed her going the opposite direction on the far side of the lake. Of course, we already knew he went for his run.”

Which was true. A cook in the dining hall reported seeing Patrick jog past the building early Sunday morning. She said he ran by almost every morning, but she remembered Sunday in particular because he seemed to be staring back through the glass with a wistful smile on his face. She told the police that his smile made her feel young again, with all the promise of youth brimming inside.

So, this new information didn’t really provide any further leads, nothing to grant a broader picture of what may have happened to Patrick. They knew he had gone out for his run that morning, and they now knew he made it at least to the far side of the lake. What they didn’t know was what had happened to him after that. It appeared that he never made it back from his run.

“What about the cell phone company?” Robert asked. “My cell phone always seems to know where I am. Surely they should be able to track him through his cell.”

“They aren’t receiving a signal from his cell,” Mrs. Young said, her voice despairing and choked.

“What does that mean?”

Another beat of silence then, “They say that means his phone has either been turned off since Sunday morning . . . or it has been destroyed.”

Now it was Robert’s turn to be silent as the implications of this weighed down on him. He started to speak, his voice broke, he cleared his throat and started again, “Maybe I can meet up with you and Mr. Young this afternoon and we can—”

"I don't know about that, we'll have to get back to you," Mrs. Young interrupted. "Now if you'll excuse me, I really have to go. Call me if you hear anything, and I'll do the same."

Before Robert could respond, Mrs. Young disconnected the line.

Stuffing the phone back in his pocket, he saw that he had wandered up near James C. Furman Hall. Robert stepped under the portico that stretched along the side of the building and started down the covered walkway, mulling over the conversation that had just ended.

Like every conversation he'd had with Mrs. Young since Patrick's disappearance. He knew the Youngs had come to Greenville and were staying at a hotel, but he hadn't seen them. He hadn't spoken to Mr. Young at all, and all his conversations with Mrs. Young were tense and abrupt. Nothing of the warmth and friendliness he'd once felt from them.

Of course, they were terribly upset and rightfully so, but he got the impression it was more than that. He sensed a coldness from Mrs. Young that felt personal, and the fact that Mr. Young hadn't bothered to speak to him also felt personal. As if they blamed him for their son's disappearance.

Not in the sense that Robert had done something to Patrick, but as if his influence on their son had somehow led to Patrick going missing. That didn't make much sense, but grief and fear did not necessarily go hand in hand with logic and reason.

As he came to the end of the portico, he angled off to the right, headed toward the auditorium. His stomach grumbled, but he didn't even consider going down to the dining hall or even the bookstore to buy a snack. He wanted to avoid Furman Lake, didn't even want to look at it. Whatever had happened to Patrick, it happened somewhere around the lake. Robert felt too emotionally raw to deal with that right now; it would be like visiting a loved one's grave.

Don't even think that! There's no evidence to suggest Patrick is dead!

True, but likewise there was no evidence to suggest he wasn't. It didn't seem possible he could have simply vanished off the face of the planet, unless he was abducted by aliens or yanked up to Heaven in a Rapture of One. So where could he be?

The lake. You don't want to consider the possibility, but it's the most likely scenario. The police know it too. It's only a matter of time before they bring men out to drag the lake.

Robert wished he could silence that voice in his head, if for no other reason than the things it had to say bore the ring of truth to a degree. He couldn't bear that at the moment. He would rather prefer a little kind of self-deception. Maybe a soap opera scenario where Patrick suffered from amnesia and had wandered into a community of Quakers and had started a new life, but soon he would begin to regain his memories, just bits and pieces at first but then a flood, and he'd return to Robert and they'd embrace and kiss to swelling orchestral music before fading to commercial.

A ridiculous fantasy. No one watched soap operas anymore.

He took a seat on the top step that led up to the auditorium's entrance, letting his head hang between his knees. He closed his eyes and tried to picture Patrick's smiling face, the smooth curve of his back, the pink tip of his tongue that he'd pinch between his teeth when deep in thought. Anything but the gently lapping waters of the lake.

Yet that was the only image his mind projected on the backs of his eyelids. Furman Lake. The thing was not a natural lake but something man-made, created sometime in the 1950s when the campus moved to this stretch of land from its original downtown location. At its deepest, the lake was only about six feet, but high bacteria counts kept people out of the water. Not likely that Patrick had decided to take an early morning swim.

But that didn't mean he didn't end up in the water. He could have fallen, hit his head and slipped into the lake. Or something more nefarious, something a cinderblock chained to his ankle.

Robert rubbed his hands roughly across his face, realizing his imagination was veering again into soap opera territory. Yet stuff like that did happen. Any day of the week you could find such stories in the news. You were horrified, but you didn't really think it could happen to someone close to you, that it could touch your life. He now understood that all the people in those horrible news stories had thought themselves immune as well . . . right until the moment they realized they weren't.

"Well, look who's moping on the steps," said a familiar voice from behind Robert.

He grimaced and wished he could will himself to sink into the ground, but instead he turned to see Gary Edwards coming out of the auditorium with a nelly queen who had played Link in the school's production of *Hairspray*. Apparently Gary's latest flavor of the month. Hell, that was being generous. More like his flavor of the week, or possibly even hour.

"Getting into acting, Gary?" Robert said. "If you have enough talent maybe you can at least *act* like you're a decent human being."

Gary leaned against one of the building's brick columns with his arms folded, his trademark cocky grin tilting his lips like a seesaw with a fat kid at one end. "Such bitterness and vitriol. Very unbecoming. Then again, what else can one expect from the recently dumped."

The nelly Link snickered behind his hand.

"What the hell is that supposed to mean?" Robert asked, getting to his feet.

Gary held up his hands as if in surrender, the seesaw smile not faltering. "I heard Patrick ran off and left you, that's all I'm saying."

"He's *missing*, you dickwad. The police are involved."

"Wow, when you get dumped, the guy doesn't play. Maybe he's in some ex-boyfriend Witness Protection Program or something, living under a new identity."

Link snickered again, standing close enough to Gary that their arms brushed.

"What is wrong with you?" Robert said. "You're like a combination of Scarecrow and Tin Man, born without a brain or a heart. Something terrible might have happened to Patrick, a man who you once dated."

"Don't remind me. He was a lousy lay, but then again, so were you."

More laughter from Link, and Robert turned his

bourgeoning fury on the man. "Yuck it up, you piece of shit actor. He'll be saying the same thing about you in a week after he's dropped your ass after fucking all your friends."

"I'm not a piece of shit actor, my performance in *Hairspray* was singled out for praise in the *Paladin*," Link said, ignoring everything else Robert had said.

The seesaw on Gary's face evened out. "Look, Robbie, I can see you got your panties all in a bunch over this, probably imagining him being kidnapped by gangsters or sold into white slavery or some such shit, but I'm just trying to reassure you that it's probably nothing as dramatic. You might not want to face it, but seems to me you've been ghosted."

Of course, Robert knew what it meant to be "ghosted." It was the term used when a person didn't have the balls to break up with you to your face, and instead simply stopped taking your calls or texts, deleted you from their social media accounts, and left you to get the hint on your own. He even had to admit to having ghosted a few guy himself freshman year. He wasn't proud of the fact, it was a particularly despicable way to go about ending a relationship.

"That's not what this is," Robert said, though his voice lacked fire. "This isn't a matter of him not answering my messages. He's disappeared from campus, his parents haven't heard from him, there have been no transactions on his bank account or credit card since Saturday."

Gary shrugged as if Robert had described a mystery as inconsequential as who ate the last slice of pizza in the box. "Like I said, when you get dumped, the guy doesn't play."

The fury continued to build and expand and bubble until it could be contained no longer. He wasn't really aware of his fist lashing out until it connected with Gary's jaw, almost as if his arm had developed sentience and acted of its own accord. It happened so fast Gary didn't have time to duck or even cry out. He took the hit full on the chin and fell back, sliding off the column and landing on the steps, rolling down to the flagstones at the bottom. A purple welt the shape of a kidney bean rose just to the left of Gary's mouth, which, for once, had been wiped clean of its perpetual smirk.

"Are you fucking insane?" Link squealed and ran down the steps to Gary, kneeling next to him and helping him up to a seated position. "You okay, sweetie?"

Gary rubbed at the back of his head then turned his attention to Robert, hell burning in his eyes. Robert immediately tensed, both hands balling into tight fists, as he felt the electrical charge of a storm about to break.

With a ferocious roar, Gary leapt to his feet and bounded up the steps, his head down and shoulders squared as if he intended to tackle Robert. Gary was taller and more muscular, in better shape and unquestionably stronger than Robert, but Robert had sheer weight on his side and he knew his only defense was to use that to his advantage.

When Gary was only one step away, Robert lunged forward, his feet actually taking air, and he struck Gary in the chest, sending them both flying back toward the ground. Gary landed on his back with Robert on top of him. As Gary tried to recover his breath, Robert reared up, straddling him, and punched the man in the face. Once, twice, and a third time for good measure. The pain in Robert's hand was extreme, as if he'd tried to punch through a brick wall, but the crunch of Gary's nose and the feel of his cracking teeth and the spurt of his hot blood were all satisfying to a degree he'd be ashamed to admit to later.

He'd pulled his fist back for a fourth punch when suddenly Link jumped on his back, locking an arm around his throat. Robert stood up, easily taking the skinny theater student with him, wearing Link like a backpack. Robert grabbed the arm choking him, and then leaned forward. With a shrug, he heaved Link off him and onto the ground.

Gary had rolled over and pushed up onto his hands and knees. He spit blood and shards of splintered tooth onto the pavement. "You motherfucking psychopath! I'm going to get your ass kicked out of school. You'll be lucky if you don't end up in jail. That's unprovoked assault, and there's a dozen witnesses to testify to that fact."

Until he said that, Robert hadn't truly been aware of the crowd that had started to gather around the front of the auditorium. Students and even a couple of professors, standing and staring, their eyes glazed with shock and the faint light of excitement often present in a crowd during a fight.

Robert's fury drained from him, as if a cork had been pulled from the bottom of his foot, letting it all escape onto the pavement. His hand was bloody and bruised and started to swell, and a deep shame replaced the fury that had driven him to violence.

It wasn't that he felt sorry for Gary. The asshole

was scum, Robert couldn't understand how he'd ever found him attractive, and he hid his own insecurities by lashing out at others with cruelty. He was pathetic. The things he'd said were hurtful and nasty, but Robert realized his attack of the other man had little to do with his verbal barbs and more to do with Robert's own feelings of inadequacy and helplessness. Patrick was missing and there seemed to be nothing he could do. He'd needed something concrete to hit in order to regain a sense of power.

He'd felt it momentarily, but that power was fleeting and left him more empty than before. While both Gary and Link cursed him and the gawkers looked on, Robert turned and fled back toward his dorm.

CHAPTER FIFTEEN:
VENTURING OUT

PATRICK AWOKE SUDDENLY, his head snapping up. There was no moment of blissful disorientation when he thought he was in his bed in the dorm, his biggest worry being that he might be late for class. He knew instantly where he was and how dire his circumstances were.

Clare slept next to him, her head still on his shoulder. His entire body felt like one big cramp, though the worst of the stiffness and pain resided in his neck and lower back. He gently pushed the girl to the side so that she slumped against door, her chin touching her chest. He rose slowly, his muscles feeling atrophied, as if he'd been immobile in a coma for months or years, his joints creaking like rusty hinges. His left arm was partially numb, beginning to buzz with the pinprick sensation as blood returned to the limb. He turned his head far to one side then the other, trying to work out the soreness. His spine felt compacted, an accordion that had been squeezed in. He walked down two steps and stretched his arms straight overhead.

"How long were we asleep?" Clare asked from behind him.

Patrick turned to see her massaging her own neck. "I don't know," he said, which was true. They could have been asleep for fifteen minutes or fifteen hours; it was simply impossible to tell. However, he felt rested and his stomach so empty that he found himself regretting that all the dog food was now on the other side of the door, suggesting they'd been asleep for a while.

Long enough for the poison to have worked?

Bounding back up to the landing, he placed his ear to the door. Only quiet greeted him. He forced himself to wait at least five minutes. Still nothing but silence. He tried to temper the hope that bubbled up like carbonation in a shaken soda by reminding himself that before he and Clare had opened the basement door, alerting the dog to their presence, they'd not heard a peep from the animal. That didn't mean it wasn't there.

Patrick balled a fist and held it up, preparing to knock on the door, but Clare grabbed him by the wrist, staying his hand. "What if he's out there?" she hissed.

"That's what we need to find out. If the poison didn't work, we need to know. If I bang on the door, if the dog is still standing it will come running and barking. Then we'll know we have to go back to the drawing board."

"No, not the dog. *Him*. Big Daddy. What if he came back while we were sleeping?"

Patrick considered this for a moment, and then shook his head. "No way. Even if the dog isn't dead, he'd have seen the bucket and the spilled dog food out in the hallway. He'd already know we were out of our cells."

Clare maintained her grip on his wrist another moment before letting go. "Yeah, I guess that makes sense."

"But we don't know when he might be back, which is why we need to move as fast as we can. Agreed?"

She managed a weak smile. "Agreed. No giving up, right?"

"You got it."

Patrick began beating on the door, and Clare joined him, and they both began yelling. After several minutes of this they stopped and both pressed the sides of their heads against the wood. Patrick kept his ears attuned for the slightest sound. A snarl, the click of nails on the linoleum, a wheeze.

Nothing, an absence of sound so total it was almost like going deaf.

"You get back down to the bottom of the stairs," he said to Clare. "Get the two-by-four and be ready. You know, just in case."

Clare nodded, and to her credit did not hesitate, though he could see her shaking as she made her way back down the stairs. Once she had the two-by-four back in her hands, Patrick turned to the door and gripped the knob.

He paused and closed his eyes. He wasn't a praying man, but he took a few deep breaths and tried to empty his mind, not worrying about the past or the future, trying to be fully present in the here and now, a few calming techniques he'd picked up from Buddhist meditation. When he felt his heartbeat settle to a more or less normal rhythm, he opened the door quickly and stuck his head out, prepared to duck back in and slam the door if the dog pounced.

He immediately saw he had nothing to worry about.

The Doberman lay on its side halfway down the hallway, its muzzle leaking a frothy white foam as well as blood. It looked like milk and tomato juice mixed together. A trail of bloody stool streaked the tiles, weaving and twisting as if the dog had run around in circles while excreting, apparently having lost the ability to control its bowels. Part of Patrick felt guilty. Other than the occasional insect, he'd never caused serious harm to another living creature in his life. Certainly never killed a living creature.

This is different, he told himself. *This was self-defense, a life or death situation. Special circumstances, the usual rules don't apply.*

He knew this to be true, but still that pang of guilt still twisted at his heart.

"The coast is clear," he called to Clare. "You can come on up."

She ascended the stairs slowly, not letting go of the two-by-four. Patrick opened the door wide and stepped into the hall, but Clare hesitated on the landing. He felt time weighing heavy on him, but he didn't rush her. He simply held out a hand. With a look of commendable resolve, she reached out with one hand to take his, the other gripping the beam as if she meant to snap it in two.

When she spotted the dog, she made a choking sound that was part gasp and part gag. But she didn't look away. Patrick had to admit that the girl was tougher than he'd first given her credit for.

"It would have torn us apart given the chance," she said, as if somehow sensing Patrick's nagging remorse. "We really didn't have much of a choice."

He appreciated her use of the word *we*, taking responsibility out of his hands alone, and he likewise appreciated her efforts to quell and comfort.

Patrick nodded and squeezed her hand before letting it go. "Okay, let's get the fuck out of here."

They went down to the end of the hallway, skirting around the dead dog. The stench was overwhelming, and Patrick placed a hand over his mouth. They paused at the T-juncture. To their right, the intersecting hall continued a short distance before turning again to the left, destination unknown. To their left, the intersecting hall opened out into a small, neat kitchen. Patrick went that way, and Clare followed.

The kitchen was a small square with a tiny alcove in the far right corner that contained a table and chairs. A breakfast nook, some might call it in a less depressing place. The room was clean but dingy, everything outdated. The floor was a gray tile that may have once been white around the time the first Bush became president, the wallpaper a yellow that might have been cheery when first installed, but had faded to the color of depression. The refrigerator and stove were about thirty years out of date, the fridge humming loudly and rattling as if in death throes. The porcelain sink was empty and dry, but rust stains blotted it like a bad case of psoriasis. The ceiling was lined with florescent tubes. Patrick didn't bother turning them on. There was enough light filtering in through the narrow window above the sink. Light as dingy as the rest of the room. Through the smudged glass the day looked overcast and foggy. There was no phone anywhere he could see.

Patrick took note of all of this in a handful of seconds, but then his attention turned directly to the door next to the breakfast nook. He hurried to it, grasping the knob and twisting. The door wouldn't budge. Then he noticed the deadbolt lock a few inches above the knob. One without a thumb-turn to unlock it, but one that could only be opened with a key, even from the inside. The door had no glass panels but was a solid slab of heavy wood.

Clare stood next to him, studying the lock herself. "Can we do like we did with the door in the basement?"

"Wouldn't work. Not only is this door much thicker than the one in your cell, the lock isn't in the doorknob. Even if we could remove it somehow, that won't get us out. We would need the key for this door."

"What about the window?" she said, already clambering up onto the counter next to the sink, still clutching the two-by-four in one hand as if afraid to let it go.

Patrick walked over, knowing that the window was not an option. Narrow as it was, Clare was slight enough that she might be able to slip through . . . except for the bars on the outside of the window. The girl seemed to notice this as she slid the window up in the sill, and she slumped with her feet in the sink.

Glancing out the window, Patrick took in the view. Not that there was much to see. Some open land, mostly dirt but with some patchy weeds and wild onions growing here and there. About fifteen feet away, trees crowded together, the beginning of a wooded area. None of it looked at all familiar to him, but a single word popped unbidden into his mind.

Isolated. The house in which they were being held was isolated. Patrick couldn't hear anything to suggest they were near other people. No cars, no televisions, no children playing, no dogs barking. They seemed to exist in a bubble, cut off from the rest of the world, drifting in a universe apart. The fog that undulated on the other side of the glass only served to increase that perception.

At that moment the silence was broken by the grumbling of Patrick's stomach. A loud, insistent growl. He turned and walked over to the refrigerator, opening it to see what was inside. Not much to see, but not empty either. A jar of pickle chips that contained mostly juice with a few chips floating around like rafts, half a loaf of bread, a few slices of cheese in their foil wrappings, a nearly full two-liter of off-brand soda. He started opening the cabinets, finding a tin of crackers, a box of Corn Flakes cereal, and a can of almonds. He gathered this all up and took it over to the table in the nook.

"What are you doing?" Clare asked, hopping down off the counter. "Shouldn't we be getting the hell out of dodge?"

"We will, but we need to eat something first."

"We don't have time for that."

"I'm not suggesting we cook a four-course meal and set the table," Patrick said, "but we need all the strength we can get, so let's scarf some of this down so we don't fall out when we need to be hauling ass."

What he didn't tell her was that his sense of urgency was leaving him. If the kitchen was this secured, chances were slim they'd find anything less in the rest of the house. He suspected the front door would also have a deadbolt that required a key, and that all the windows would be barred from the outside. Of course, he could be wrong, but that seemed unlikely, and if he was right, then why not delay the crushing disappointment for a few more minutes.

Whether she detected his doubts or not, she joined him at the table, leaning the two-by-four against the wall. They began to tear into the food. She started on the pickle chips and Patrick the crackers. They were slightly stale but he didn't mind. At this moment they tasted like filet mignon. The faint saltiness was like a drug, and he actually moaned as the crackers turned soggy on his tongue and he swallowed the wad with an audible *click* in his throat.

Both he and Clare turned to the cheese next, cramming the slices into their mouths. As she moved on to the almonds, he turned his attention to the bread. A few of the slices were rashed with mold, but he just ate around it. He washed it all down with three huge gulps of the soda, which was as flat as the Midwest, but to him was as sweet as nectar from Heaven.

"I better slow down," he said, breathing heavily and leaning his palms on the tabletop. "I don't want to make myself throw up, but it all tastes so fucking good. I'm so glad I held out and didn't resort to eating that dog food."

In his periphery, he saw Clare suddenly stiffen and he suddenly realized his mistake. "If you had been here as long as I have, you'd have eaten it, too."

"Clare, I didn't meant to—"

"It's just like what you had to do to the dog, you know. Not something you wanted to do, but something you *had* to do to survive."

"I know," Patrick said, putting a hand on her shoulder, feeling the tension in her body. "I didn't mean to say you'd done anything wrong. Truth is, you're stronger than me, you have a stronger survival instinct. I admire that."

This seemed to placate her. What he said was partially true. The girl had some steel in her, he couldn't deny that, yet he also couldn't deny being somewhat disgusted knowing she'd chowed down on dog chow. Yet she was right, you did what you had to in order to survive.

"Can we get out of here before Big Daddy gets back?" she said.

Patrick nodded, threw a handful of almonds in his mouth, and then crossed to the counter by the stove and pulled a butcher knife from the cutlery block. "You want one?" he asked.

"No, I'm good," Clare answered and retrieved the two-by-four.

They followed the hall to the end and took the left turn, passing three closed doors without pausing to investigate them. This hallway opened up to a larger living room. Furniture was sparse, a sagging sofa with a scratched coffee table in front of it, a rickety bookcase that held a few moldering paperbacks as well as a collection of clown figurines. As if this whole scenario couldn't get any creepier. The walls were white and bare, no pictures or prints, though a few cleaner squares suggesting some had once been hung. Patrick did a quick search, and while he found two phone jacks, there were no phones plugged into them. Part of him was not surprised; it couldn't be that easy.

The room had two windows with no curtains or blinds, and Patrick could clearly see the bars on the outside. He went to the door, found it as thick as the one in the kitchen with the same type of deadbolt. Just as he had suspected. He tried the knob anyway, then beat his head gently against the wood a few times out of frustration.

Clare had gone to the window next to the door, staring out. "I don't even see a road."

Patrick joined her and saw a wide front yard with a dirt drive that stretched out several feet before entering another copse of dense trees and disappearing altogether. There was no way to tell how far they were from a main road.

Clare flopped down on the sofa, the beam laid across her lap. "What do we do now? Check the other rooms, see if there's an unbarred window or a phone?"

"We can, thought it seems unlikely. Maybe we can break the glass out of one of the windows and see how secure the bars are. Perhaps we can somehow pry them loose from the outside of the house."

Without a word, Clare stood, walked over to the window along the side wall and smashed the glass with the two-by-four. She skipped backward as some of the shards rained down on the hardwood floor. A few more swings and the frame was devoid of all glass.

"How's that?" she asked, glancing over her shoulder with a faint smile.

With a smile of his own, he crossed over to the window. Now that they were out of the basement, all her earlier trepidation and uncertainty seemed to be dissipating, revealing an admirable determination and resolve.

Patrick reached through the opening, a warm breeze wafting in to brush against his sweaty face, the first fresh air he'd felt since his run around the lake however many days ago that had been. He had lost track. The bars were cool and he shoved against them, hoping for some give. There was none.

"Want me to take a whack at them with this?" Clare said, holding up the two-by-four. She seemed to have become incredibly attached to it. He'd thought of it as a weird security blanket earlier, and he didn't think that was far off the mark.

"I don't think that'll do it, not for these bars. They're pretty firmly bolted. I know it's a longshot, but maybe somewhere in the house we can find a crowbar or something we can use to—"

He stopped speaking abruptly as a soft sound drifted to his ears. At first he thought it was the sighing of the wind, but as he turned his head he realized it was coming from somewhere inside the house. A soft humming, a familiar tune. A lullaby, not "Rock-A-Bye-Baby" but something he knew. Maybe "Hush Little Baby." Yes, that was it.

"We're not alone," he said in a whisper. The humming was faint, definitely feminine, almost soothing in nature. The humming then turned to actual singing.

"Hush little baby, don't say a word. Mama's gonna buy you a mockingbird . . . "

Clare wandered toward the hallway. "That voice . . . I know it . . . "

"Where are you going? We don't know who that is."

Ignoring him, Clare started down the hall and

Patrick felt he had no choice but to go after her. They tracked the humming to the third door on their left. Patrick gripped the knob and gave Clare a meaningful look. She seemed to understand, as if they had developed a form of telepathy, she nodded and raised the two-by-four like a club.

He turned the knob slowly and pushed the door in. It opened slowly, with a slight creak, revealing a cramped bedroom with only a strained mattress on the floor, no sheets, and no other furniture except a wooden rocking chair by the window.

A woman sat in the rocking chair, early 50s if Patrick had to guess, her graying hair loose and disheveled. She was thin, wearing only a light pink nightgown. She stared out the window, through the bars, not turning her head in their direction, continuing to sing the lullaby.

Clare stepped over the threshold. Patrick grabbed her arm but she shook him off.

"Linda?" she said in a tentative voice. "That's your name, right? I'm Clare, I was in the room next to you in the basement. Do you remember me?"

Finally the woman turned her head. Her eyes were vacant for a moment, as if looking into a void of nothingness, but then she seemed to register the two newcomers and her lips spread in a grin. "Why, hello, dear."

Clare glanced back at Patrick, and with their newly developed telepathy, he read in her expression the message, *I don't think she's all there.*

"Are you okay?" Clare asked, inching closer to the woman. "I didn't know what happened to you after he . . . took you away."

"Oh, I'm fine," Linda said, reaching out toward Clare, her eyes looking past the girl to meet Patrick's gaze. "It's so nice of you two to visit me. My sweet children."

CHAPTER SIXTEEN:
LINDA'S ABDUCTION

WHEN LINDA CHILDERS *heard the* ding *of the microwave, she carefully placed a bookmark in the Ruth Ware paperback she was reading and got up from the cushy recliner, leaving the book on the end table. In the kitchen she took her Banquet meal out of the microwave, sitting it on the counter to cool for a few minutes, while she made herself a cup of herbal tea. She placed the meal and her teacup on a tray and carried it all back to the living room. Settling on the sofa, she placed the tray on the coffee table in front of her. She turned on the television and found a rerun of* Murder She Wrote *and began to have supper.*

This was a nightly ritual, though aspects of it changed. Sometimes her frozen meal was lasagna, other times macaroni and cheese, still other times beef stroganoff. The television program varied, depending on what was on, but it was typically some rerun, since she didn't find most modern shows appealing. If not Murder She Wrote, *then* Touched By an Angel *or* Doctor Quinn, Medicine Woman. *An old sitcom like* I Love Lucy *or* The Andy Griffith Show *would do in a pinch. She'd watch until she finished her meal and then she'd resume reading. This she would do until she was ready for bed.*

Linda's house was filled with books. Overburdened shelving units lined the walls, but they were unable to contain her collection. Books were stacked up all over the place, creating literary towers that she would weave through as if a labyrinth of knowledge. Books were Linda's passion, and in them she found a portal to other realities. She could live other lives, be other people, have epic adventures and torrid romances and thrilling battles. To the outside world she was what her grandmother would have called a spinster, a forty-three year old woman who'd never been married and hadn't even been on a date in the last ten years, no children and no close friends, spending all her time either at the library where she worked, walking at a nearby cemetery, or here at home. Yet in her mind, she was so much more. Hero, villain, lover, all these things and then some.

None of it was real, of course. She knew that; she wasn't crazy. But when she was swept up in the story, it felt real. Certainly realer than her routine life. Realer and certainly safer. She knew some of the younger girls she worked with at the library thought she was sad and they pitied her. Let them. Meanwhile, they would continue getting their hearts broken, becoming more bitter as the hurt built up like a wall, creating a prison brick by brick.

Of course, Linda was walling herself up book by book, but she viewed the books as doorways, representing freedom, not entrapment.

A gunshot on the screen made Linda jump and she

realized she'd been sitting here for several minutes, lost in her own thoughts. Her dinner was cooling, and she wasn't sure exactly what was happening in the episode. Someone was dead, the police were clueless, but Jessica Fletcher could be counted on to figure it all out in the last fifteen minutes or so.

Focused on the narrative once again, Linda took a bite of the now-lukewarm lasagna. In moments, however, her mind began to drift again. This often happened when watching TV. The visual medium simply did not hold her concentration as well as the words on a page.

Books were her passion. So much so that as a younger woman she'd entertained dreams of being an author herself, creating those worlds to which others could be carried away. She'd written a lot of poetry, several short stories, and made more than a few attempts at novels, though she'd never completed one. In the end, she'd given up the dream as unrealistic. Her grandmother would have said she lacked stick-to-itiveness, and it was possible that was part of it, but mostly it was realism that caused her to abandon that pursuit. She recognized she lacked the talent to be a truly great storyteller.

And so she'd become a librarian, surrounding herself with the books she loved but could not craft herself. It was a compromise, but one she could live with.

She was halfway through her meal when she heard a knock at her front door. The sound was soft and tentative, but Linda jolted as if a gun had been fired right next to her head. Some of the lasagna dropped from her fork and hit her cream-colored *carpet. Normally, this would have left her distraught, her being a woman who believed that cleanliness wasn't next to godliness but actually above it. Yet she barely noted the cheap tomato sauce seeping into the fibers, her attention focused on the door.*

The knock came again, light but insistent. Linda felt frozen, gripping the handle of the fork, her heartbeat loud in her own ears. She recognized how silly it was for her to react to a simple knock at her door as if it were a harbinger of doom. For someone else, it might be nothing, just a friend dropping by for a casual visit or a neighbor wanting to borrow a hammer or screwdriver.

But Linda wasn't someone else. She was only herself, and she didn't have friends to drop by and she didn't even know her neighbors' names. John Donne had famously said that no man was an island, but Linda was living proof that some women were.

So who could be at her door at half past eight on a Wednesday evening? The answer was unfathomable to her.

Only one way to find that answer.

She stood, realized she still clutched the fork like a weapon and placed it in the square plastic container of lasagna. She moved slowly toward the door. There had been no further knocking since the second bout, and she wondered if whoever had come knocking had given up and left, presuming her not to be home despite the fact that the TV could surely be heard on the front porch.

Four squares of glass made up the top portion of the door, covered by a frilly lace curtain. She pulled this aside and peered out onto the porch. She saw a shadowy shape standing back from the door, the broad shoulders indicating a man. The head was turned, as if he were looking over his shoulder back toward the street, perhaps debating whether or not he should leave.

Linda considered ducking away and letting the curtain fall back into place, but before she could move, the man faced forward again. Spotting her, he stepped forward until the light from the living room shone through the glass and illuminated his smiling face.

She was surprised to discover she recognized that face and that smile. But instead of bringing clarity, recognition brought more confusion.

"What . . . what are you doing here?" she said through the glass.

The man pulled in his chin, a blush coloring his cheeks. "I'm sorry. I know this is so forward of me, showing up on your doorstep when we haven't even exchanged names. Do you remember me . . . from the graveyard?"

Linda nodded. Of course, she remembered.

She lived on Drace Avenue, right next to the Mountain View Cemetery. It had become a routine for her to walk there for an hour every evening after work. If it rained, she took an umbrella, in the winter she bundled up, during a heatwave she took a bottle of water and kept well hydrated. The walks were good for her body, helping with her circulation and cholesterol, but they were also good for her mind. Walking helped elevate her mood and made her feel that she wasn't so much of a recluse, even if she usually had the cemetery to herself.

Until recently.

About a month ago, she had found herself sharing the graveyard with this gentleman. He would typically show up ten to fifteen minutes after she began her walk, traversing the small lanes that cut through Mountain View, turning the land into a grid. Another person using the cemetery as a track. He never walked as long as her, staying only half an hour before leaving. They would pass on occasion, exchanging smiles and a pleasant, "Good evening?" or "How do you do?" Nothing more, but Linda would be lying if she had said she'd never sensed a certain shy flirtation in the man's smile. Just as she'd be lying if she didn't admit that his smiles filled her with a certain warmth.

For the past week, she had actually been trying to work up the nerve to strike up an actual conversation with him, but the fear had been great and kept her silent. She was too old for flirtation, and she was definitely too old for what that could lead to.

Yet she had started touching up her makeup and primping her hair before her walks.

"How did you know where I live?" Linda asked, glancing around the room for her purse. Her cellphone was inside.

"I wasn't spying on you or anything, I swear. One day last week during your walk, you came over into this yard and picked up some trash and threw it away. I figured this must be your house. That's all."

It made sense, but that didn't make his appearance any less strange or unsettling.

"What are you doing here?" she asked again. "It's very late."

"I know, I know, I shouldn't have come. I should have asked you out nice and proper earlier when I saw you at Mountain View, but I chickened out and I've been kicking myself ever since. I was at home, consuming a little liquid courage quite frankly, and I figured I should just walk right over here and do it before I gave myself time to chicken out again. But I see now it was a mistake, and I just look like some kind of stalker freak. I'm sorry, I didn't mean to disturb you."

He turned and started across the porch, and Linda moved without thinking, acting on pure instinct. Instinct and a latent loneliness bigger than she had previously realized. She unlocked the door and opened it. "Wait, I didn't . . . I mean, you don't have to go."

He paused, and turned back, pulling his chin in again. "I really am sorry. I'm exhibiting atrociously bad manners."

"Don't be silly," she said, stepping through the door and holding out her hand. "We haven't properly met. My name is Linda."

He took her hand in a semi-firm grip and shook. "Bill."

"Nice to meet you, Bill. I assume you live around here. At least within walking distance, that is."

"Um, yes, I live out near Poinsett Street," he said, gesturing vaguely toward the downtown area. "Relatively new to the neighborhood."

Linda nodded, and then the two of them stood facing one another in silence. She felt awkward, oddly gangly, but a buzz of excitement tingled across her skin like a low electrical current. The *feeling was familiar but distant, and it took her a moment to place it. This was the feeling she'd gotten as a girl when in the presence of a boy she liked, a boy she suspected might like her back, and neither one of them could seem to think of anything to say.*

"Okay," Bill said after taking a deep, fortifying breath. "I walked over here for a reason, so I should get to it. Linda, would you like to go out to dinner with me some night?"

She hesitated. Not because she didn't want to say yes immediately, but because the fact that she wanted to say yes immediately frightened her a bit. Fact was she had considered the concepts of dating and sex as things of the past, a part of her life that was over. She thought she'd made peace with that, had done away with any romantic notions, but apparently they were not gone, only suppressed.

Yes, there was the excitement of meeting someone new, learning his story, sharing yours, the thrill of kissing and groping and discovering one another's bodies. She was smart enough to know that part didn't come by itself, however. Along with it, there were disappointments and fights and silent treatment and emotional blackmail.

But not every relationship ends up that way, *she told herself. Sometimes it seemed that way, but she had known couples that seemed genuinely happy. True, those seemed the exception rather than the rule, but you would never know if you could be one of those exceptions unless you took the chance.*

"I'd love to," she said, and the electrical tingling increased when she saw the relief on Bill's face.

"I'm so glad. Maybe I can get your number, call you up and make plans."

Linda hesitated again, but it passed quickly. She felt suddenly daring, not her usual self but one of the heroines in the romance novels she sometimes read. Someone who was confident and took risks and was sometimes even brazen.

"Would you like to come in for a moment? I could make us some tea and we could talk for a bit."

Bill looked back at the street as if trying to decide whether he should, but then he turned a bright smile on her and said, "I'd love to."

She stood aside and let him enter in front of her, feeling simultaneously bold and foolish. Inviting a strange man into her home at such a late hour. Although she reminded herself that it wasn't really all that late. Not for most people. 8:30 would probably be considered quite tame by most people's standards, in fact.

"Lovely place," Bill said as Linda closed the door. She realized how pathetic the setup made her look. A frozen meal for one, the flickering light of the television, and a single lamp in the corner providing the only illumination.

A nervous titter of a laugh escaped her. "You know what they say, be it ever so humble. I'll go fix you a cup of tea."

"Thank you, but you don't have to go to the trouble. Drinking tea at this hour would probably keep me up."

"It's caffeine-free."

"Yes, but it would have my bladder going all night."

"Oh, of course," Linda said, taking the remote and turning off the television. This of course cut the light in half, a gloom descending. "Would you like to just sit and talk a while?"

"Very much."

She took a seat on one end of the sofa and he the other. She wouldn't have minded if he'd sat closer to her, but she also appreciated the fact that he was gentlemanly enough not to presume.

"Are you new to Greer?" Linda asked when the silence started to stretch out.

"Oh, no, lived here my whole life."

"I see. So you recently moved into this neighborhood then?"

"Um, yes. That's right."

"Welcome to the neighborhood," she said then winced at her own weak attempt at humor. "Sorry, I'm just a bit nervous."

"Oh, I'm in the same boat. I've been wanting to talk to you for some time, but I needed the moment to be right."

Linda smiled and looked down into her now room-temperature tea. "That's very sweet."

"From the first moment I saw you, I knew you were the one."

She continued staring down into her cup, a crease forming between her eyebrows as a slight frown twisted her lips. "The one." That was laying it on a bit thick. Of course, so was showing up on her doorstep uninvited.

Seemingly oblivious to her sudden discomfort, Bill continued unabated. "I was instantly drawn to you, I think because of your resemblance to my wife."

Now Linda's head jerked up and her frown deepened. "Your wife?"

"My late wife. She passed a long time back now, but she's never left my heart. You look so much like her. Not identical or anything, but there is a resemblance. It makes me feel almost like she has been returned to me."

Linda found this turn of the conversation more than a little uncomfortable. The man saw her as simply a replacement for his deceased wife. A stand-in. There was nothing appealing about that.

Bill must have sensed her discomfort, because he said quickly, "I know I'm saying all the wrong things. I tried to plan out a whole speech on the drive over here, but once we were face to face, it got all jumbled in my head. I'm sorry, your beauty turns me into a blathering idiot."

She felt herself beginning to respond to the flattery, but then her mind seized on something else he'd said. "The drive over here?" she repeated. "I thought you said you walked over."

This seemed to fluster Bill, and he stammered a moment before saying, "Well, I walked over from the graveyard. That's where I parked my car."

A chill worked its way down her spine like a trickle of ice water, and she found herself scanning the room again for her purse. "Why would you do that? Why not just park at the house?"

"We wouldn't want the neighbors to talk, would we?" he said with a smile that no longer looked charming or playful, but somehow predatory.

The kitchen. Linda suddenly recalled that she'd left her purse on the kitchen counter.

"You know, it's getting late," she said. "I'm quite tired. Maybe we can continue this conversation another time."

Bill didn't move, merely sat there with that creepy grin on his face. "Now that I've found you again, I won't let you go. I promise this time I'll take better care of you, and nothing will be able to part us."

When Linda inhaled, the air sliding down her windpipe felt arctic, freezing her from the inside out. This situation had ceased to titillate, and now all she felt was a burgeoning terror. If this was one of the mystery novels she often read, she would have rolled her eyes at her own actions, considering herself an unbelievably dense character to have let a virtual stranger into her house because she was lonely.

"If you'll excuse me," she said, rising to her feet and holding her cup with both hands to keep it from shaking, "but I want to freshen up my tea. I'll only be a minute."

She started toward the swinging door that led into the kitchen, trying to keep her movements casual, nothing to betray the panic that made her want to dash into the other room. Despite her efforts, every step felt awkward and disjointed, like she were a newborn just learning to walk.

She quickened her step as she approached the door, eager to get to her phone and call the police. Maybe it would turn out she was overreacting, that Bill was nothing more than a harmless albeit odd man with even fewer social skills than Linda, but she would rather be embarrassed than murdered in her own living room.

Her right hand was reaching out, preparing to

push open the door, when an arm hooked around her throat from behind. She let out a startled gasp. She hadn't even heard him following behind her; apparently he moved with the stealth of a ninja. She tried to jerk away, but he tightened the chokehold, cutting off her air. She attempted to scream but couldn't get enough oxygen. Her fight or flight reflexes kicked in, and since flight wasn't an option, she began bucking and twisting, kicking back and reaching behind her to scratch at his eyes.

Nothing she did seemed to have any effect on him, as if he were some inhuman machine out of one of the Terminator movies. No matter how hard she struggled to free herself from his grip, the arm around her throat felt like a vise. She felt her heel connect with his shin but he didn't budge, didn't even grunt. Her fingers couldn't find his eyes, but her fingernails drew trenches in the flesh of his cheeks. This did not deter him or make him loosen his hold.

Linda tried desperately to get air into her lungs, but Bill had effectively cut off her trachea. Her desperation grew more furious as black spots began to bloom in her vision. Instead of trying to pull away, she pushed back, hoping to catch him unaware and topple him, causing him to let go in the fall. It seemed almost as if he'd anticipated this move, and he merely took a step back then began lowering himself to the floor, taking her with him.

"Don't worry," he whispered into her ear. "I'm not going to kill you, just need you to go to sleep for a little while. I am going to put you somewhere safe, protect you, and we'll have the life we should have had. This

time we'll even have children. A girl and a boy, I think. It'll be perfect this time around."

Linda's movements had become sluggish, the black spots spreading until they were a film that covered over most everything else, blotting out the world. Her mouth opened and closed like a fish out of water, drowning in a sea of oxygen. In her mind's eye, she conjured an image of that suffocating fish, and how she envied it.

"I love you so much," Bill said, his words tender and soft, which made it all the more horrifying. As if he thought choking her in her own living room was somehow a romantic gesture. "You are my wife, and Big Daddy will take good care of you. The world won't be able to touch us or ever separate us again."

She cast her eyes around the room, catching glimpses through the eclipsing film, and the last thing she saw before unconsciousness claimed her was her copy of the Ruth Ware, the bookmark sticking out one third of the way through.

I'll never get to find out how it ends, *she thought,* before the black film covered over everything.

CHAPTER SEVENTEEN:
MOMMY DEAREST

"**I THINK I** know her," Patrick said.

Clare glanced back at him. "Really? You do?"

"Not personally or anything, but she looks so familiar. I think I remember seeing news stories about her disappearance."

Turning her gaze to the woman once again, she scanned her features to see if they sparked any memory, but there was nothing. Not surprising. Clare didn't pay much attention to the news, local or global, and that had become even truer since she started dating Hank. She could admit that she had turned into one of those girls who thought of nothing but her relationship, doodling hearts with arrows through them and writing her first name with his last name. Silly high school stuff from a girl who claimed not to believe in fairytales but still expected her life to turn out like one.

Even after she'd been abducted, such fantasies persisted. After all, most fairytales had a dark period before the happily ever after. Cinderella had to flee the ball, Snow White ate the poisoned apple, but the

Prince always showed up at the end to rescue the damsels in distress. She spent many hours curled up on the cold floor, imagining Hank busting down the door, sweeping her into his arms, and carrying her out of this hellhole.

Of course, she knew better now. Life wasn't a fairytale; it was a horror movie. One of those extreme, violent torture porn ones. She'd been tempted to revert to her childish way of thinking when Patrick beat his way through the wall and into her cell, but he wasn't a prince or a knight or the hero of some paranormal YA romance. He was just a man, practically a boy, with determination and a survival instinct honed sharp as a knife.

And she was just a girl who had let fear cripple her. Inspired by Patrick's determination, she could gather her strength and courage and be the hero of her own story.

Except those torture porn movies never have true heroes and usually only work out well for the villains.

She gave her head a vigorous shake, trying to dislodge these intruding thoughts like a dog shaking off fleas, and refocused on Linda. The woman seemed to have forgotten they were in the room again, staring out the window and now humming the tune to "Twinkle, Twinkle, Little Star."

"Do you think they've made the connection?" Clare asked Patrick.

"What connection?"

"Between our disappearances. I mean, three people from the same areas going missing. Do you think they're investigating them as separate cases or they suspect we were all taken by the same psychopath?"

Patrick stepped next to her. He had the knife held down by his side, the tip pointed at the floor. "I don't know. I mean, it's possible, but you have to also consider that our disappearances were spaced out. The authorities might not see a pattern in them."

"What about her? How long do you think she's been here?"

Patrick didn't answer right away, and she could see in his eyes that he was debating whether or not he should tell her the truth. She couldn't blame him. She'd acted like a total scaredy-cat freak earlier, resigned to rot in that cell forever. She'd given up, but now she was getting her second wind.

Perhaps he sensed this new resolve because he said, "If memory serves, I saw those news stories about her nearly a year ago."

Fresh horror washed over Clare and she had to blink back tears. "A year? She's been here for a year? He's been doing . . . those things to her all that time? No wonder she's gone batty."

Linda seemed to become aware of them again, and she locked eyes with Clare. Only there was nothing in that gaze, just a vacant void. "My girl, why do you look so sad? Don't fret, Big Daddy will be home soon, and maybe he'll bring an ice cream treat. Won't that be nice?"

Feeling helpless, Clare turned to Patrick, but he didn't seem all that interested in Linda. He was inspecting the room's one window, barred from the outside like all the others. Clare gently placed the two-by-four on the floor and knelt down next to the rocker, taking one of Linda's hands in both of hers.

"Linda," she said softly. "My name is Clare, Clare Barrett. Do you know where you are?"

The woman's lips spread in a smile as vacant as her stare. "I'm home, silly."

"Where are you from originally?"

"Here. I've always been here."

"No, you haven't," Clare said, squeezing the woman's hand as if she could lead her wandering mind back to reality. "You had a life before this. Try and remember."

Patrick was rummaging through the drawers of an old, weathered dresser with a cracked mirror. He turned to Clare and asked, "Did you have your cell phone on you?"

She glanced over at him, her mind a jumble of confusion. Too much for her overloaded brain to process, and she suddenly wanted to follow Linda down whatever rabbit hole she'd fallen into. "What?"

"Your cell phone," Patrick said again, speaking slowly as if to a dim-witted child. "Did you have your cell phone on you when you were abducted?"

"Oh, um, yeah, I did."

"So did I. There's at least a chance they could be somewhere in this house. If we can find them, we can call for help."

"But we don't even know where we are."

"Doesn't matter. They'll be able to trace the signal and find us."

Of course, that made sense. If Clare weren't so frazzled, she would have thought of it herself. "What about her?" she asked, inclining her head toward Linda.

"She'll be fine. She's in her own little world."

"Yeah, I know, but don't you think we should try to snap her out of it or something?"

Patrick came to her and placed a hand on her shoulder. "Clare, I think it's going to take a lot more than a conversation to snap her out of this. She seems too far gone."

"Can't you do something? You're majoring in Psychology, after all."

He gave her a look of such heartbreaking sympathy that she again felt like a dim-witted child. "I'm only a second year undergrad. I'm not exactly Carl Jung over here. She seems to have slipped into a dissociative state where the trauma she's experienced has made her lose touch with who she really is. If I had to venture a guess, I'd say the only way she could cope with what has happened to her is to give in to the fantasy created by her abductor. That she is his wife, that we're just some happy family. If she's ever going to recover from this, she'll need extensive therapy."

"If? You mean, there's a chance she might not recover?"

"I don't know, Clare. Like I said, I'm just a student. Now come on, help me look for our cell phones. The sooner we find a way out of here, the sooner we can get Linda some help."

Linda had gone back to staring out the window, her hand in Clare's completely slack. It was like holding a dead bird. She had retreated back into herself, but Clare spoke to her all the same. "Linda, we're going to try and find a phone. We'll be back. I promise we won't leave you here."

She didn't respond, but Clare patted her on the hand as she stood. She picked up the two-by-four and she and Patrick started from the room. At the door, she heard Linda mutter behind her, "Big Daddy doesn't let us talk to other people. He says when you have your family, you don't need anyone else."

Clare paused for just a moment in the doorway, and then followed Patrick out into the hall without looking back. There were two closed doors remaining in the hallway. Pointing to the one on the left, he said, "You try that one. I'll try the other."

"Do you really think it's such a good idea to split up?"

"You have your club and I have this," he said, holding up the knife. "Scream if you find any skeletons in the closet, figuratively or literally."

She felt herself begin to tremble at the prospect of leaving Patrick's side, even if only for a few moments. Only moments before she had thought she had found her strength, but that was on the surface. Deep down, a scared little girl still cringed in the corner of her cell.

"It's okay," Patrick said, reading her fear and reaching out to take her hand. "I'll be right over here, just a few quick steps away. You can do this."

She lifted her chin resolutely.

Patrick held her hand for a moment longer then let go, turning to his door. Clare took a deep breath then clutched the knob of hers and pushed open the door, stepping inside.

It was dark, and a suffocating sense of claustrophobia crashed in on her like a black wave. She fumbled on the wall to her left then the right, finally finding the light switch and flipping it, a dim, yellowish light drifting down from a ceiling fixture with a dirty cover that filtered out more light than it let through.

She found herself in a small, cramped bathroom, not much longer than one of those old-time phone booths Superman would have changed in back in the day. To her left was a water-stained toilet bowl; to her right was a small sink with a medicine cabinet above it; straight ahead was a claw-footed tub with a shower curtain that encircled the entire thing on a metal track. The tile was a dingy black-and-white diamond pattern.

She used the two-by-four to reach out toward the shower curtain. Her imagination conjured an image of Big Daddy lurking behind the curtain, ready to jump out like some demonic jack-in-the-box. Such a scenario didn't make much sense, but that didn't seem to lessen the fear that took hold of her heart with icy hands. Bracing her feet slightly further than hips distance apart, she used the beam to shove the curtain aside in one quick, fluid motion.

For an instant, she thought she actually saw Big Daddy there and she lunged forward, the two-by-four passing through nothing but air. The tub was empty, rust surrounding the drain, a rigged showerhead attached to the shower curtain frame above the faucet.

Clare planted the beam on the floor like a cane and allowed herself to slump forward, relief making her feel weak. A shuddering laugh escaped her and she turned to the medicine cabinet, the only place in the windowless room for her to search. The mirror was spotted and streaked, obscuring and distorting her reflection but that suited her fine. She probably didn't want to know exactly what she looked like.

She glanced back toward the shower, thinking how good it would be to strip out of these disgusting clothes and stand under the spray, allowing all the filth and grime of the past few months to wash off her body. She could practically feel the warm water cascading down her skin, and an orgasmic chill worked its way through her.

Unfortunately, she realized time was too short for such luxuries, tempting as they might be. She did take a moment to run cold water into the basin of the sink and splash it onto her face. Then she opened the medicine cabinet, revealing three metal shelves containing only a stick of deodorant, a nearly empty tube of toothpaste, a toothbrush with frayed bristles, and a comb missing a few teeth right at the center. Nothing more, nothing useful. Not even so much as a straight razor that could be used as a weapon in a pinch.

She scanned the room one last time for anything she might have missed. Other than a few folded towels on the back of the toilet tank, the room was bare. She turned off the light and went back out into the hall. She glanced into Linda's room. The woman leaned forward in the rocker, staring toward the door, wringing her hands. "Big Daddy will be back soon," she said, her voice strident with anxiety. "We should wait for him to get home."

"With any luck, we'll be long gone before he gets back," Clare said. "Try not to worry. We're all going to get out of this."

Clare left the doorway and went to the third room. The door was ajar and she walked into another bedroom, this one slightly larger than Linda's and with more furniture. A bed with an actual frame, a chest of drawers and two storage trunks. Patrick had tossed the mattress off the frame, all the drawers in the chest were open, their contents strew about the floor, and he was currently hunkered down next to one of the trunks, rummaging through it.

He looked up when he became aware of her in the room. "Find anything?"

She shook her head. "It was just a tiny bathroom. Thought I'd see if I could help you."

"I haven't checked that closet in the corner yet."

"I'm on it."

Leaning the two-by-four against the wall, she opened the closet door. She'd thought the bathroom was the size of an old phone booth, but this closet truly was. A rod along the top supported a dozen wire hangers from which nothing hung. The floor contained one pair of heavy, dirt-encrusted steel-toe boots and one worn blue bedroom slipper without a mate. She turned her attention to the shelf up near the top of the closet.

She had to stand on her tip-toes and stretch in order to reach. Her hands flailed around until they landed on something. She pulled down an old shoe box and removed the lid. She stared down into the box for a few moments, her expression blank, before finally turning toward where Patrick was now digging through the second trunk. "I found our phones," she said in a breathy whisper.

Patrick hurried over, nearly tripping over the detritus from the trunks. He snatched the box from her hands and reached inside, pulling out Clare's Kyocera and an iPhone she assumed belonged to him. He let the shoebox tumble to the floor, holding the phones, one in each hand, frowning at them as if they were puzzles he could not solve.

Clare could sympathize. She knew what she saw, but it wasn't what she wanted to see. The shattered screens and cracked casings, as if someone had taken a hammer to the phones. Which was probably exactly what Big Daddy had done. Though it seemed futile, Patrick attempted to turn the phones on anyway. With the expected success, which was to say none.

Time seemed to stop for a moment, suspending them in a pocket universe outside the normal flow, and Clare found herself holding her breath, as if afraid this universe contained no oxygen. In contrast, Patrick sucked in a deep lungful of air but he didn't release it right away. He just kept drawing in breath, and Clare began to worry he wouldn't stop until he suffocated on it.

But then he did release the breath, released it as a primal scream of frustration and anger and despair, so loud and raw that Clare actually put her hands over her ears. Patrick tossed the phones into the closet, where they struck the back wall and came apart into several pieces. He dropped to his knees, his scream dissolving into huge, wracking sobs. He hugged himself and shivered as if he'd been caught outside in frigid weather.

Clare hesitated a moment, and then dropped down next to him and draped an arm across his shoulders. The force of his sobs caused her own body to vibrate as well. She patted him on the shoulder and said, "It's okay, it's gonna be okay," rather embarrassed by her lackluster comforting skills.

"It's not okay. This whole situation is pretty fucking far from okay."

This latest disappointment seemed to be the metaphorical straw that broke the proverbial camel's back, and Clare felt there had been a shift, a role reversal of sorts. Now Patrick was the basket case and she was the strong one. She didn't feel completely comfortable in the role; it fit like a pair of pantyhose one size too small.

For a few minutes, they didn't speak. He continued to cry, and she continued to hold him and pat his shoulder. She couldn't think of anything else to say but figured that was probably for the best. Her father was wont to say that sometimes sharing a meaningful silence with someone could be more therapeutic than a dictionary full of empty words. She'd always rolled her eyes at that particular bon mot, but now she saw the wisdom in it.

Gradually, Patrick's sobs tapered into weeping and then into sniffles and a few stray tears. With his eyes squeezed shut, he took several deep breaths then wiped the slug trails off his cheeks and she could feel the shift again, the balance restoring itself.

"I'm sorry," he said. "I lost it there for a minute."

"You don't have to apologize to me. I'm the original hysteric. I'd say we're both entitled to a freak out or two."

"We may be entitled to them, but we can't really afford it," he said. "If we don't get out of here before the sonofabitch comes back . . . well, it will be bad."

Clare glanced over at the two-by-four, chewing on her lower lip. "What if . . . "

He followed her gaze. "What if what?"

"When he gets back, he won't have any way of knowing we've gotten out of our cells. At least not until he gets into the house. We could use that to our advantage."

A smile flickered across Patrick's lips. "The element of surprise. We could get the jump on him if we're waiting for him."

"One of us could take the front door, the other the back," Clare said, though the words scraped out of her throat like rocks. The idea of confronting Big Daddy alone filled her chest with a dread like black tar. Yet there wasn't much of an alternative as they couldn't know for sure which door he would enter from.

"Sounds like a plan," Patrick said.

"Yeah, but not exactly a *good* one."

"In our current situation, I'd say it's the best plan we have."

"Any port in a storm and all that."

"Exactly," Patrick said, getting to his feet. He stepped into the closet and grabbed hold of the rod, tugging on it. "I wonder if I can yank this out."

"Why?"

"The knife is good for close up, but between you and me and at the risk of sounding like a total wimp, I would rather not get too close up to this guy. I want something I can swing at him from a distance."

Clare was about to suggest they go back down to the basement and try to knock out another one of the two-by-fours, but Patrick had begun to wrench at the rod. It only took three good pulls and the thing came loose so suddenly that he stumbled back and landed on his bottom.

He sputtered a laugh. "With this kind of coordination and prowess, I'm sure to best any foe that comes my way."

Despite the dire circumstances, Clare found herself laughing as well. "Look at it this way, you distract him with your klutz routine, and I'll sneak up behind him and club him over the head."

"Finally, a sensible plan," Patrick said, grinning up

at her. Then he looked past her, into the closet. The grin faltered. "What's that?"

She glanced over his shoulder toward the top of the closet where his gaze was leveled. "I already checked the shelf. There was nothing there but the shoebox."

"No, not the shelf. In the ceiling."

Patrick got to his feet again and walked into the closet, holding the rod in one hand like a staff. With his free hand, he pointed up at the ceiling. "See there, that square."

Clare stepped behind him and followed his finger. She could see it, a square like a trap door.

Patrick used the end of the rod to press against the square, and it lifted up, revealing a dark space on the other side.

"An attic," he said, voice infused with a childlike excitement.

Clare's mouth and throat felt very dry, and she tried to work up some saliva but it was like trying to get blood from a stone. She'd spent too much time in a basement, she didn't like the idea of crawling up into an attic. What she wanted was the wide open outdoors.

"There could be a window up there," Patrick said, letting the square fall back into place, though slightly askew, revealing a tiny sliver of that darkness.

"Not to be all Debbie Downer, but even if there is, chances are it will be barred as well."

"Maybe," Patrick agreed. "But maybe it would be too much trouble to put the bars on a window not at ground level. It's at least worth a look."

Clare nodded, but still she dreaded the prospect of going up into a cramped attic full of cobwebs and rats and all that blackness.

Patrick turned and scanned the room. "I need something to climb on top of to get up there. Maybe I could turn one of the trunks on its side or—"

He broke off abruptly and darted from the room, as if suddenly overcome with the cramps of impending diarrhea. She followed into Linda's bedroom where he went to the woman and said in a brusque voice, "I'm going to need your chair for a minute."

Linda turned her vacant eyes to Patrick, the euphoric smile of someone high on drugs curling her lips. "There's my boy. Why don't you sit on Mommy's lap and I'll rock you to sleep."

Patrick sighed and rubbed at his temples. "Look, lady, I need the chair. Get up."

Clare went to Patrick and placed a hand on his arm. "You don't have to be so mean. Have a little sympathy. I mean, think of all she's been through."

"I know, but think of all we're going to go through if we don't get out of here."

"Let me try."

"Be my guest, but make it fast. I can practically hear a clock ticking in my head, warning me that we're almost out of time."

Clare moved to Linda and tucked a strand of hair behind the woman's ear. "Mommy, will you come play with me?"

"Wanna play patty cake, patty cake, baker's man?"

"No, I was thinking about Candyland."

"Oh, what fun!" Linda said, clapping her hands together. "Go get the board and we'll set it up."

"I already set the board up in Daddy's room. Will you come play?"

Linda stopped clapping and her hands began to

twine together to form complicated knots of flesh and anxiety. Her eyes darted to the door and she seemed to shrink in on herself even more, a turtle trying to retreat into its protective shell to hide from a predator. "When Big Daddy isn't here, I'm not supposed to leave my room except to go to the bathroom. It's one of the rules."

Thinking on her feet, she adjusted her approach. "Oh, Big Daddy is home. Came in a few minutes ago. He's waiting in his bedroom; he's going to play Candyland with us."

Her hands still twisting around one another, she said, "Really?"

"Absolutely. He sent us in here to get you. Isn't that right, Patrick?" When he didn't answer, she glared at him and repeated in a sharp tone, "Isn't that right, Patrick?"

He started as if a firecracker had gone off next to him. "Oh, yeah, that's right. We don't want to keep him waiting."

"Certainly not," Linda said, gripping the arms of the chair and pushing herself to her feet. "Big Daddy hates to be kept waiting. That's another rule."

Clare took her by the arm as if she were a decrepit octogenarian, not someone around the age of Clare's own mother. The trauma seemed to have aged her body while regressing her mind to that of a child. "I'll walk with you, and Patrick will bring your chair."

In fact, Patrick had snatched the rocker up from the back almost before Linda had even completely removed herself from it, and he was currently on his way out the door with it. Clare led the woman along, out into the hall where she clung to Clare as if they were traveling through some dark fairytale wood.

This is worse than any fairytale, Clare thought. *On the page there is always the promise of a happy ending, but real life offers no such promises.*

As they walked into the other bedroom, Patrick was already trying to wrestle the rocker into the closet. Linda frowned then looked around the room. "Where's Big Daddy? Where's the game?"

Clare firmly gripped the woman's shoulders and turned her so they faced one another then put her hands on Linda's face, one on each side, so that they stared into each other's eyes. "Linda, listen to me. We have to get out of here. Patrick is going to go into the attic and see if he can find a way out."

Linda tried to shake her head no, but Clare held it in place. "We can't leave here. It's against the rules. It's the *main* rule!"

"We have to," Clare insisted, determined to break through the woman's madness and find a core of sanity. "The man who is keeping us here is not your husband, he's not my father. I'm not your child. My name is Clare Barrett. I'm fifteen, my parents' names are Phil and Sue, and we live on Overbrook Drive in Greer. I was abducted from Greer City Park. Do you remember where you live? Do you have a family out there somewhere? Where did he abduct you from?"

"You're wasting your breath," Patrick said. He'd placed the rocker into the closet backward, so that its back was against the inner wall. "She's too far gone for you to reach her."

As if to prove Patrick's point, Linda reached up and batted Clare's hands away. "We can't leave!" she shouted, her face transforming into something vicious.

"You're trying to break up our family, and Big Daddy will punish us all for your disobedience!"

Patrick had stepped up onto the seat of the rocker, gripping the edge of the shelf to steady himself as the thing rocked gently back and forth a few times before it settled. He looked over his shoulder at them. "Will you go back to pretending we're one big happy family about to play Candyland and calm her down?"

Clare reached out to take Linda by the shoulders again, but the woman lashed out and struck Clare hard in the face, right across the left cheekbone. Pain flared in her eye like a bomb detonating in her optic nerve.

Before she could fully recover from the blow, Linda pounced on her, tackling her and driving them both to the floor, Clare on the bottom. She tried to push the woman off her, but Linda seemed possessed of the strength of a banshee, no longer a frail old woman but a primal she-beast. She straddled Clare and began striking her repeatedly in the face, screaming the whole time.

"You're a naughty girl! Big Daddy gives us a home, security, affection, and this is how you repay him? Both of you are rotten, ungrateful children! Big Daddy will be so angry! I can't let you do this, I can't let you—"

Clare got her hands up, trying to shield her face from further assault, and behind Linda she saw Patrick appear. He swung the closet rod and it struck the woman in the side of the head, cutting off her words neatly and sending her toppling over on the side, freeing Clare of her weight.

Clare rolled over and pushed up onto her hands and knees. Her face stung in many places, and she tasted blood from a split lip. She could also feel her left eye swelling, and she was sure purple bruising was already puffing up the flesh around the socket.

But she could see clearly, could see Linda lying on her side, the hair around her temple matting with oozing blood. The woman did not move.

"Oh, God," Patrick said in a choking voice, letting go of the rod so that it clattered to the floor. "I killed her."

CHAPTER EIGHTEEN:
ASHES TO ASHES

SUE BARRETT LAY in bed, resting on her left side with her back to her husband. Her body was balanced precariously on the very edge of the mattress, on the verge of toppling onto the floor. Behind her she could hear her husband snoring softly, had been listening to the sound for hours. According to the clock, it was nearing 9 a.m., which meant they'd been in bed almost four hours, and she'd been awake the entire time, watching as the darkness gradually gave way to a grainy light through the windows.

Listening to Phil's snores.

She found herself baffled that he could sleep, baffled and angry that he could find escape in slumber so easily after everything. She simply couldn't shut her mind off, thoughts churning and twisting like laundry in a dryer. Any time she closed her eyes, she saw a blaze reflected on the backs of her lids and adrenaline pumped into her system, taking sleep even further out of her reach. She groped for it, and it would shrink back away from her questing fingers.

She'd considered getting up several times, going

downstairs to find something on television or try to read a book, but in the end she couldn't muster the energy to rise. As wide awake as her brain was, her body was exhausted. Leaving her in a state of surreal horror worse than any nightmare she'd ever had.

Even now she couldn't bring herself to get up. Normally she and Phil would already be at work at this hour, but they'd both called out the night before, which wasn't unusual, not since Clare went missing, so their respective bosses were used to it. She should get up, make some breakfast, at least try to act as if everything were normal. If she couldn't do that in the privacy of her home, what hope was there she could put on such an act in public?

And despite her husband's assurances, she knew there was at least a possibility such an act might be required.

She wrinkled her nose as the phantom scents of gasoline and acrid smoke invaded her nostrils. She knew these smells were only in her imagination. Both she and Phil had showered before getting into bed, and the clothes they'd worn last night were balled up in a trash bag in the laundry room downstairs, waiting to be burned.

Burning . . . guess that's our new thing. Wonder who will get to light the match this time?

Telling herself the smell wasn't real did nothing to dissipate it. As if the fumes were now ingrained in her very skin, woven into the fabric of her being.

She wondered for the hundredth time why she had allowed her husband to talk her into doing what they'd done. Yet deep down she knew that was unfair. She'd gone along willingly, full of righteous fury and vengeful conviction. Only after they'd gotten home and were sitting in the car, the garage door rattling down behind them, had doubt and guilt crept into her mind. Doubt, guilt, and fear.

Phil had assured her repeatedly they would not get into trouble, that no one would know it was them, but how could she take those assurances seriously? He was a junior high school guidance counselor, for Christ's sake. Just because he had watched all three seasons of *Hannibal*, was she supposed to think he was suddenly a criminal mastermind?

Sue's reverie dissipated like steam when weight shifted on the mattress as Phil got out of bed. She could *feel* his stare as if it had mass as he stood there, looking at the back of her. She did not roll over but remained still, trying to make her breathing slow and even so he would think she still slept. After a moment, she heard him shuffle off to the bathroom. The house was so quiet she could hear the splash as he urinated and then the machine gun rattling of the shower.

With an annoyed grunt, she pushed herself up, throwing off the cover and putting her feet on the floor. Another damn shower, after the marathon session he had spent in there the night before. The water was lukewarm by the time she'd been able to have her turn, turning icy before she was even halfway through washing her hair so that she'd had to take a cold shower like a teenage boy when his girlfriend wouldn't put out after a heavy make-out session.

Cursing Phil under her breath, she went downstairs. She hadn't felt like putting on her pajamas last night, so after her shower she'd merely slipped into her bathrobe and slept in that. Not that she'd slept.

In the kitchen, she took a glass from the cupboard and filled it from the faucet, a gratified smile touching her lips when she heard Phil cry out as the hot water cut out on him for a moment. There was bottled water in the fridge, but she was feeling spiteful. The glass was halfway to her lips for the first sip when she heard the sound of a distant siren piercing the quiet of the night.

Suddenly shaky on her feet, she let the glass clomp down onto the counter, water sloshing over the rim. She closed her eyes and pictured a bright red fire engine, an oversized child's toy, shrieking across town. Of course, that was ridiculous. The fire had been started hours ago, it was surely out by now. Besides, the Bukharis lived all the way across town. It didn't seem likely that she would be able to hear any of the emergency vehicles from here, even distantly. In fact, she could no longer hear the siren at all. Perhaps it had never been there, a phantom sound conjured up out of her guilt and suffering just like the phantom scents.

A knock from the front of the house made her jump, her hand nudging the glass over the edge of the counter. It shattered on the linoleum. She stepped back quickly, avoiding the pieces of broken glass, but water doused her feet.

The knock came again, and she was halfway across the room before she realized she'd started moving. She felt in a dream, the familiar surroundings of her own home now alien and slightly askew, not so much walking across the floor as gliding, pulled along by some tractor beam. In the den, she paused near the stairs. She could still hear the water in the shower; Phil had apparently heard none of the commotion on the first floor.

By the time she reached the door, a third knock sounded, loud and insistent. She pressed an eye to the peephole and let out a groan when she saw a fish-eye view of her worst nightmare. A police cruiser parked at the curb, and two officers standing on the porch.

Sue gasped and took a quick step away from the door, as if afraid they could somehow see her standing at the peephole. Her heart began to trip-hammer in her chest like a heavy fist beating against the bars of a cage. She glanced back toward the stairs, wondering if she should run up and tell Phil, let him come down and answer the door.

She actually started across the room but then a fourth knock stopped her. The longer she delayed answering the door, the more suspicious things would look to the officers. They were probably already suspicious. She should answer, play it cool.

She looked down at herself, wearing only her robe. No time to change. Making sure the security chain was secured, she opened the door a few inches and put her face to the crack.

"Officers, may I help you?"

The officer closest to the door was a middle-aged guy with the square jaw and crooked nose of a cowboy from a spaghetti western. Behind him was a younger Hispanic, his face smooth and unblemished, almost like a baby's head stuck on an adult body.

The older officer said, "Ma'am, sorry if we woke you. Are you Mrs. Barrett?"

She clutched the top of the robe and thought, *Of course! Dressed this way with my hair looking like a rat's nest, it would be natural to assume they woke me. That could account for why it took me so long to come to the door. I can even use this to my advantage if I'm smart, play up the grogginess and confusion.*

"Um, yes, I am. What seems to be the problem?"

"I'm Officer Workman, and this is my partner, Officer Sanchez. Is Mr. Barrett home? We'd like to speak to both of you if possible."

"He's in the shower."

"Ma'am," Workman said, stepping closer to the door, "could we come in? We have some questions for you and your husband."

"Do you . . . ?" she started, meaning to finish with *have a warrant*, but she clamped her mouth shut on the question. That sounded like exactly the kind of question a guilty person would ask, and she didn't want to appear guilty. If they did have a warrant then she couldn't keep them out anyway, and if they didn't then even if she let them into the den, they couldn't just go romping through the house without her consent, not without probable cause.

Or at least she thought that was how the law worked.

"Do you want something to drink?" she said to cover.

"No thank you. I promise we won't take up much of your time."

Clare closed the door, undid the chain then opened the door, trying to plaster on a pleasant smile. But not too pleasant. She reminded herself they were invading her home. She should be polite, but there should also be a touch of puzzlement and maybe even irritation.

As the two men came inside, Sue folded her arms across her chest and glanced back at the stairs once more. She could still hear the damn water running.

"It may be a few minutes," she said with a titter. "My husband takes long showers. If you'd like, I can run up and let him know you're here."

"That won't be necessary," Officer Sanchez said, speaking for the first time. "We'll wait."

An awkward silence settled between the three of them, and Sue debated whether or not offering them a seat was something a guilty person would do. All she could think about were the stinky clothes in the trash bag in the laundry room, just through the kitchen. Hopefully the smell wouldn't carry this far. There was also an empty gas can sitting in the trunk of their Camry. She silently cursed Phil for his long showers. He should be the one down here dealing with this.

"Do you mind if we have a look around while we wait?" Sanchez said, already moving toward the archway into the kitchen.

Deciding to go on the defensive a little, Sue stepped in front of him and said, "I think I'd like you to tell me what this is all about."

The two officers exchanged a glance and Workman answered with a question. "Do you know Dr. Bukhari and his family?"

Sue's body tensed and her windpipe constricted; she sucked in breath with a rattle and a wheeze. Part of her had hoped the visit from the police was about something totally unrelated, a prowler spotted in the neighborhood or something. She tried to mask her sudden dread and got her breathing under control before responding. "I'm familiar. The Bukhari boy goes to school with our daughter."

One of Sue's self-imposed rules was they never spoke of Clare in the past tense. Not the Bukhari boy *went* to school with her, but he *goes* to school with her. Of course, Sue realized the pretense was useless. Everyone in the police department knew the girl was missing, just as they surely knew by this point that Phil and Sue suspected the Bukharis were behind the disappearance.

"Well," Sanchez said, "their house caught on fire last night."

Sue was horrified by how close she came to saying, "No, it was only the garage." She bit into her tongue hard enough to draw blood, trying to swallow down her stupidity. She recovered quickly, hoping the horror she was sure showed on her face was taken for horror at what had happened.

"Their house caught on fire?" she repeated as if the words didn't even make sense to her. "Is . . . I mean, was anyone hurt?"

She knew the answer from Workman's grave expression even before he spoke. "Yes, ma'am. Dr. Bukhari and his wife suffered mild smoke inhalation, but their son Hank . . . "

The officer trailed off, leaving Sue in excruciating suspense. She felt herself trembling, her entire body quaking as if in the grips of a severe chill. "What . . . is he . . . how bad is it?"

"He has third degree burns all down the right side of his body."

"The fire started in the detached garage," Sanchez continued. "But it was a windy night. Fire jumped over to the back corner of the house. Right where Hank Bukhari's bedroom is."

"Any idea how the fire started?" she asked, trying to sound casual. "Bad wiring or something?"

"Suspected arson," Workman said, his gaze steady on her. "The garage went up so quickly, there had to be an accelerant involved. Plus, the neighbor that lives behind the Bukharis saw a car in the alley between their properties shortly before the fire started."

"A car?" she said, the world seeming to collapse in around her so that nothing existed but her and Workman. Even Sanchez dissolved into the background.

"That's right. Due to a bout of insomnia, Mrs. Keller was up watching TV. She thought she heard an engine and went to look out the backdoor. She saw a dark Camry idling in the alleyway then taking off. Just after that, she noticed the flames. She called 911 right away, but as I said, the garage went up fast, and by the time the fire trucks arrived, the house had already caught as well."

Clutching the robe near the throat, she sank down onto the ottoman. "Camry, you say?"

"Yes. I believe Mr. Barrett has a 2014 Toyota Camry registered in his name. Is that correct?"

Sue didn't answer. She thought of every generic cop show she'd ever seen on television. *You have the right to remain silent.* Good advice, though perhaps it was a little late to take it at this point.

"Mr. Keller also managed to remember that the license plate number on the car in the alley ended with 502. According to DMV records, your husband's license plate number is DME 502."

"There are at least three traffic cameras between the Bukhari residence and here," Sanchez said. "We've requested the footage from all three and should have that to review soon."

Still, Sue said nothing, but her mind turned to the intersection of Wade Hampton and Highway 14. When Phil had seen the traffic light turn yellow on the way home last night, he'd sped up but the light had definitely been red when he'd zoomed under it.

Workman towered over her, looking more like Clint Eastwood in *The Good, the Bad and the Ugly* than ever. "Do you have anything you want to tell us, Mrs. Barrett?"

At that moment, she heard the gurgle as the water in the shower was finally turned off.

"No, I have nothing to say," she said and waited for her husband to come downstairs.

CHAPTER NINETEEN:
THE ATTIC

"**I KILLED HER**," Patrick said again, dropping to his knees. Distantly, he heard Clare saying his name, but it was small and tinny, as if coming through a radio with a bad connection. Or as if he were at the bottom of a deep well and she were calling down to him from the top.

All he could think about at the moment was the fact that in a matter of a few hours, he had killed first a dog then graduated to killing another human being. Acts of which he would have thought himself incapable of a mere week ago.

While Patrick didn't go so far as to actually call himself a practicing Buddhist, he did have great respect for their philosophies and had spent some time visiting with a Buddhist monk at the Cambodian wat in Wellford. One of the things that resonated the most with Patrick was the Buddhist belief that all life was precious. Not just human life, but all life. Buddhists tended to be vegetarians and didn't wear leather, but it went even deeper than that. The monk he met literally wouldn't hurt a fly, and that was literally in the literal sense of the word. Flies, cockroaches, rats, ants, snakes, even mosquitos . . . the elderly Cambodian man in the orange robes had said he would intentionally harm no creature great or small. Most people would think that was insane, letting bugs and rodents scurry around your home, but Patrick found something beautiful in such an extreme respect for life.

Or so he'd thought, before he'd become a canine killer and a murderer. And while an argument could be made in both cases for self-defense, murder was what it felt like to him. Deep down, where the ugly truth often lived.

"I killed her," he continued to say, over and over like audio on a loop. "I killed her, I killed her, I killed her, I killed her."

Clare knelt in front of him but he couldn't focus on her face, the dimensions blurred. She spoke to him, but the words were so muffled and garbled he couldn't make out the sense of them. He saw her raise her hand but wasn't sure why until he felt the sting of the slap across his cheek. Just like in the movies when someone was hysterical.

And just like in the movies, it snapped him out of his reverie and brought him back to himself. Clare's face came into sharper focus and he could understand her words when she said, "Patrick, she's not dead."

"What?"

"Linda's not dead. You only knocked her unconscious. Look, you can see she's breathing."

Patrick turned his attention to the woman lying prone on the floor. Clare was right, her chest rose and fell in a steady rhythm, and he could even see that her eyes moved rapidly beneath her lids as if she were in the midst of a dream. Hopefully one a million times better than her current reality.

A shudder of such profound relief passed through him that he collapsed down to his hands and knees and choked out a few sobs before regaining his composure. "I didn't want to hurt her," he said. "I mean, she's a victim like we are. I didn't want to hurt her."

Clare gently put her fingers under his chin and forced him to look up at her. She seemed suddenly more mature than before, and he could see the woman hiding inside the girl's features, just waiting to break out like a butterfly from a cocoon.

"You saved me," she said. "Linda isn't in her right mind, and I feel terrible for her, but the bald truth is she was hurting me and likely would have hurt me much worse. You stopped her. Thank you."

Patrick took a depth breath and nodded, his gratitude toward her in this moment overwhelming. He grabbed the discarded closet rod and used it as a cane, pushing back up to his feet. Gingerly, he lifted Linda from the floor and laid her down on the bed. The mattress seemed lumpy in places, springs poking up in others, but it had to be marginally more comfortable for her. Impulsively, he delivered a soft kiss to her forehead.

"Okay," he said, turning back to Clare. "Let's check out the attic."

Back at the closet, Clare held the rocker as steady as she could as Patrick climbed onto the seat once again. He used the rod to lift the square and push it to one side then slid it through the opening. He then reached up and planted his hands on the attic floor, pulling himself up and through. While he was an accomplished runner, his upper body strength wasn't as impressive, and by the time his head cleared the opening, his arms were trembling like cornstalks in a strong wind.

He flashed back to Junior High, when he'd still been a scrawny, skeletal kid. His father called him String Bean, and his mother called him Ichabod for reasons he never fully understood. Despite his gangly appearance, he'd been a fairly decent athlete, particularly good at basketball and soccer, but the bane of his existence was when they would be expected to do chin-ups in gym class. He would be lucky to make it up to the bar once; most often he'd merely dangle there for a moment or two, straining and grunting and on one embarrassing occasion breaking wind with the force of a cannonball exploding out of a cannon, until finally he'd have to let himself drop back to the floor and feel all the stares weighing down on him, none more heavy with judgment than the stare of Coach Barrymore, his eighth grade gym instructor. Barrymore had been harder on Patrick than anyone in the class, calling him pansy and lightfoot and sometimes just Patricia. It had gotten so bad that halfway through the school year his parents had gone to talk to Principal Willis. Patrick had been pulled out of that class but there had been no actual repercussions for the coach. Years later, when Patrick had gone to his first gay club, he'd only been mildly surprised to run into Barrymore there. Typical self-loathing technique, attack in someone else the qualities you despise in yourself.

Thinking about all of Barrymore's taunts and jabs sent a shot of adrenaline through Patrick's system, boosting his energy so that he pulled his body through the opening up to the chest, his elbows snapping out to either side and pounding down on the wood of the attic floor. Bearing down on his elbow, he pulled himself further until he could hinge at the waist and lay his entire upper torso on the dusty floor and crawl along until his legs were also through the opening.

He lay there for a moment, letting his breath fall back into its normal rhythm, then raised his head to scan his surroundings. The attic was large but the ceiling was low, maybe five feet from floor to rafters, not even enough space for Patrick to stand upright. Except for a few boxes, a stack of old yellowing newspapers tied with twine, and what at first he took for some rusty fencing that he eventually recognized as a dissembled dog kennel.

He could see all this because of the sunlight filtering through a round window straight ahead. He stared at the window for a moment, stared through it to the outside world. An unencumbered view. No bars.

No bars.

"Clare, get up here," he called.

"Take this," she said, and the top of the beam poked up through the opening. Patrick took it and placed it next to the rod. He scooted around so that he was looking back down into the closet. Clare clambered up onto the rocker, taking a moment to get her balance as it creaked back and forth.

On his knees, Patrick held his arms down through the opening. "Come on, I'll help you up."

She stretched her arms and he clamped her wrists in his hands, tugging her upward. She was surprisingly light, and he nearly fell backward as she shot up into the attic. They both landed on the ground with weak laughter.

"Sorry," Clare said. "Should have resisted more."

"It's fine," he said, getting back to his knees and pointing toward the window. "Look."

Clare gasped when she saw the unbarred window, and in her excitement tried to stand but banged her head against one of the rafters. Crouching lower, she hurried across the attic and Patrick followed. In places, the wood beneath his feet bowed as if rotten and he thought they should be more cautious, but with possible freedom so close, caution seemed akin to folly.

They made it across without crashing through to the rooms below and dropped to their knees. The window was roughly the size of an 18 wheeler's tire, the glass at least an inch thick and dirty, but Patrick could clearly see out to the front of the house, the drive that led into the wooded area. He was not high up enough, however, to see above the tree line, so he still didn't know how far they were from a main road.

"I think God's finally smiling down on us," Clare said. When Patrick glanced at her, he saw her forehead was pressed against the glass and she was staring down. He followed her gaze and saw exactly what she meant.

If he had to estimate, he'd say they were fifteen feet up from the ground, not the same as diving off the Empire State Building or even a bridge, but still plenty far enough to do some serious damage.

Yet just below them, about seven feet down, was an overhang that Patrick assumed jutted out over the front porch. They could drop down onto that and from there only eight feet to the ground. Definitely doable, almost as if the universe had provided them with stepping stones to freedom.

All that stood in their way was the thick glass. The window did not open out or up; the only way through it was *through it*.

Patrick started beating on it with the closet rod, and Clare followed suit with the beam. They kept it up for almost five minutes before Patrick dropped the rod and bent forward, panting with his hands on his thighs.

Clare also stopped, sitting with her back against the wall next to the window. "Glass is too thick," she said between gulping breaths. "I guess I spoke too soon about God smiling down on us."

"Any god that would allow things like this to happen to people like us is not anyone I'd ever want to meet."

"What now?" she asked.

The only response he could give was to hold his arms out and shrug, a gesture both helpless and hopeless. For every obstacle they encountered, another one merely cropped up. Even if he did figure out a way through the window, they would probably then discover the property was bordered by a twenty foot high electric fence or something. He supposed they would have to revert back to the plan of waiting at either entrance to the house to surprise Big Daddy whenever he returned.

But what if he doesn't? What if something happened to him, or he merely left us here to starve to death?

Clare pushed away from the wall, a smile flickering across her lips. "I think I have an idea."

"Really? What is it, make me mad, see if I turn into the Hulk?"

"We're gonna chisel our way out," she said then started back toward the opening down into the closet. She'd made it halfway when her left foot punched through the rotten wood and her leg disappeared almost up to mid-thigh. She cried out as her right leg went out from under her, going straight out like she was doing a half-split.

Patrick started to rush to her but then forced himself to go slow, testing every step before putting his full weight down. Eventually he went down on all fours and crawled the rest of the way to her.

She was crying and trying to get her right foot back under her.

"Stop," Patrick said and she froze. The wood around her leg was splintered and jagged; he was afraid if she tried to pull her leg out, the edges would dig into her flesh. Her jeans were ripped and he could see blood. Not a lot, but some. "Are you hurt?"

Clare sniffled a few times and wiped the tears from her cheeks. "Not really, mostly startled, but I seem to be stuck."

Patrick studied the wood around Clare's thigh. Seemed if he could just remove a couple of large chunks, she would be able to slide her leg back out without any threat of further injury. He reached out but then stayed his hand, looking up at Clare. "I'm going to try not to hurt you."

She stared back, her gaze steady and resolute. "I trust you."

It was a tight squeeze, but he managed to get a few fingers between the wood and her leg, and he tried to pull back then up. Clare winced and sucked air in through her teeth, but she didn't cry out and she remained still. It didn't take much pressure for the wood to give and snap off. He crept gingerly around her, removing smaller bits of wood then one larger chunk at the back of her leg. This created enough of an opening that she was able to scoot back and pull her leg out of the hole.

Patrick examined the leg. The jeans were ripped in half a dozen places, the skin broken and blood seeping out of several cuts and abrasions, but nothing too severe or deep. Could have been worse. Much worse.

"You scared me to death," Patrick said with a shaky laugh. "Where were you going in such an all-fire hurry?"

Clare prodded her wounds, her expression suggesting she was surprised to find her leg still attached to her body. "I was going to go down and search the house for a screwdriver and a hammer."

Patrick remembered what she said a moment ago about chiseling their way out, and if life were a cartoon, a lightbulb would have illuminated above his head. "That just might work. Instead of trying to shatter the whole thing, we start smaller, create a bunch of fine cracks right in the center, and then we might be able to bust through."

"That's the idea."

"Okay," he said. "Sounds like a plan, but you stay here and I'll go down and look for a screwdriver and hammer."

"I can go with you. It's not that bad."

"Don't argue with me. We're about to have to climb down out of here, and then run who knows how long to find help. Better you rest the leg while you can."

For a moment it seemed she was going to argue but then she nodded.

"I'll also see if there's any kind of antiseptic in the bathroom."

"I didn't see any, but there are some towels."

"Got it. Try not to move around too much up here and I'll be back in a jiff."

CHAPTER TWENTY:
RISE AND SHINE

SHEILA RAMSEY WAS the nurse on duty when Bernie Wilson woke up.

She wasn't supposed to be. Teddi Gibbs was on the schedule, but she claimed to have come down with some kind of stomach bug and said she couldn't possibly come to work. Janice had pulled Sheila in because technically it was one of her on-call days.

When the phone rang at six this morning and Sheila had squinted at the caller ID to see the hospital's number, she'd been tempted to ignore the call and let it go to voicemail. In fact, the first time she didn't answer, but then thirty seconds later the phone started to ring again and with a groan and a curse, she'd snatched up the phone and barked a bristling, "Yeah?"

And now here she was, working a twelve hour shift when she'd stayed out at the Gaslight Bar near the airport until they closed at 2 a.m. She was exhausted, hung over, and plotting a million different ways to torture Teddi. At thirty-nine, she simply didn't bounce back from a night of partying like she used to.

Of course, Shelia had been known to call off work

at the last minute from time to time, and not always for reasons entirely on the up-and-up. Just last month she'd called out with a migraine, but in reality had simply decided to take a daytrip up to Brevard, North Carolina. Also, no one had forced her to go out when she knew she was on call the next day. Instead of giving her perspective, however, this only solidified her assumption that Teddi was also faking it to play hookie and she became even more irritated.

She went about her rounds grumbling under her breath, snapping at CNAs for things not their fault, and even losing her patience with sweet Mike Hardison. She hadn't even been in to see Gloria Richardson yet because if that bitch daughter of hers gave her any grief, Sheila didn't trust herself not to haul off and smack the ever-loving shit out of her.

Instead, she went to check on Mr. Wilson. There was a patient guaranteed not to push her buttons. Hard to get aggravated by a turnip-head.

Of course, as soon as she walked into the room, she realized she was wrong. The stench of excrement alerted her to the fact that the comatose man had soiled his adult diaper again. Great, just what she fucking needed. Her head was pounding, her mouth felt as dry as the Sahara, she could barely keep her eyes open, and now she had to clean up after this gork.

If it were near the end of her shift, she would be tempted to pretend she didn't notice and leave it for the night nurse to take care of, but as her shift was only beginning, that wasn't really an option.

Not that she didn't consider it.

With a weary sigh and a mental curse that all of Teddi's hair and teeth should fall out, she went over to the counter by the sink, donned some gloves and gathered up some wipes and another adult diaper. She pulled down the top sheet to see if anything had leaked out but saw nothing. Which meant his bowels must have emptied relatively recently.

She considered just changing his brief herself, he was light enough that she thought she could manage, but she reminded herself that patients being fed intravenously tended to have extremely watery stool.

She stuck her head back out in the hallway and saw Belinda, an older nurse a few years from retirement, coming toward her. "Hey, Bel, would you mind helping me change this guy's brief?"

A younger nurse would have probably wrinkled his or her nose, make a comical gagging sound, but Belinda's expression did not change as she veered toward the door. Shelia had to hand it to those old-timer nurses; they'd seen and done everything, and almost nothing fazed them.

"Our resident Rip Van Winkle," Belinda said as she went around to the other side of the bed.

Shelia frowned. "Who? Is that the guy in that Halloween story about the horseman with a jack-o'lantern head?"

"Never mind," Belinda said as she shut off the feeding pump, lowered the head of the bed then raised the mattress up so they wouldn't have to crouch down to change him.

After lifting the patient's gown, Sheila grabbed the edge of the Chux Pad under him and lifted it up, causing him to roll over onto his side. Belinda caught him and held him in place as Sheila removed the soiled diaper and wiped him down, applying the thick pink barrier cream to his bottom that she always thought was the consistency of a partially melted milkshake. After tucking the new diaper up under him, she and Belinda reversed positions, Belinda pulling up her side of the Chux Pad and Sheila holding him in place. The older nurse finished cleaning him then pulled taut the diaper and they lowered him down onto it. They weren't perhaps as gentle as they could have been, but it wasn't as if the guy could complain with his brains turned to mashed potatoes.

"Need anything else?" Belinda asked, peeling off her gloves and disposing of them.

"I'm good. Thanks a lot, Bel."

The older nurse nodded, and then left the room. Belinda started fastening the new brief, musing about what you could get used to if exposed to it long enough. When she'd started working at Pelham as an RN, she'd never even changed a baby's diaper and the first time she had to clean an incontinent patient, she'd almost vomited. Now she did it without batting an eye. It still wasn't pleasant by any stretch of the imagination, but she'd gotten used to it.

Like the fat stub of the gork's erection that poked up at the ceiling as she closed the brief. Once such a thing would have made her blush, but after seeing so many patients' boners, she'd become immune to it. Just another biological response.

Sheila pulled the gown down then lowered the bed. When she glanced up at the man's face and saw his eyes wide open, staring back, she was so surprised she actually screamed and stumbled back a step.

His gaze left hers and darted around the room. He licked his lips and said in a hoarse croak, "Where am I? What's going on?"

At first, Sheila was too stunned to speak. She couldn't have been more shocked had she seen a ghost or a unicorn or a single straight man in his forties that didn't chase after girls half his age.

Belinda rushed back into the room. "What's wrong, girl? I heard you holler."

"He . . . he's awake," Sheila said, pointing toward the bed.

Belinda didn't scream but her normal poker face slipped and her mouth hung open like that of a broken Nutcracker. "Good Lord," she said.

Sheila made a conscious, concerted effort to regain control of herself. She was a professional, after all. "Bel, go get Janice. I'll stay here with him."

Belinda stared at her blankly for a moment, then turned on her heel and disappeared down the hall to get the Charge Nurse. Shelia walked over to the side of the patient's bed and decided to do an orientation check. Janice would do a full assessment when she got here, but Sheila could get things started.

"Sir, do you know your name?"

He frowned up at her, his eyes frightened like a child who believes a monster lives under his bed and comes out once the lights are off. "Bernie. Bernie Wilson."

"Very good. Do you know your date of birth? Do you know who the President is?"

"What are you talking about?" he said, staring down at the PICC line sticking into his left arm. "What is happening? Am I in a hospital?"

"Yes, Pelham Medical Center. You were involved in an accident."

He started to rise, but she placed a restraining

hand on his shoulder. "How long have I been here?" he asked.

"A couple of days. You were unconscious."

"I have to get home. I have to get home right now."

"No," she said firmly but not without compassion. "You need to let us take care of you."

"You don't understand, they're all alone. They must be wondering what happened to me."

"Who? Who's all alone?"

"My family," he said in a wail. "My family is all alone, probably thinking Daddy has abandoned them."

Sheila frowned. Her understanding was that the patient had no family, which was why no one had visited except the police and the man who had actually hit him. Had he suffered some sort of brain damage?

He studied her studying him, looking confused and adrift and even a bit suspicious. "Dogs," he said flatly. "I have dogs; they are like my family. With me gone, there has been no one to feed them. They must be starving to death."

Before Sheila could say anything to try to calm him down, Janice came into the room, Belinda right behind.

"Good morning, Mr. Wilson," the Charge Nurse said with a wide smile. "It's good to see you awake."

"I have to get home to my family," he said, trying to sit up again. This time it was Janice who restrained him.

Turning to Sheila, Janice said, "Go down to the nurse's station and page Dr. Bice. Get him up here right away. He'll be grumpy, he always is, but tell him I said to haul ass."

"Yes, ma'am," Sheila said. She left the room, her

hangover forgotten. Halfway down the hall, she could still hear the patient shouting.

"My family! I need to get home to my family!"

CHAPTER TWENTY-ONE:
GOING DOWN

CLARE TRIED TO turn her focus away from the pain, but the truth was her leg hurt like a sonofabitch. She could see that the cuts weren't deep and the bleeding was sluggish, the wounds already scabbing over, yet they throbbed and pulsed with living fire. She wondered about infection, but surely it would take longer than a few minutes for that to set in.

Patrick was taking more than a few minutes himself. He'd gone to search for a hammer and screwdriver at least fifteen minutes ago, she'd guess. She heard the sounds of rummaging from time to time. She also listened for the sounds of a car approaching outside.

They were so close to getting out. In a suspense film this would be the exact moment that Big Daddy would return. The fear, like the pain, burned inside her, but she tried to ignore it, to push past it. She needed to stay strong. Later, after they were through this and were safe, she could break down, but not now.

A small gasp escaped her lips when she heard a clattering to her right, but it was only Patrick tossing items through the opening, before he pulled himself up.

"You find them?"

"Sorta," he said, crab-walking over carefully. He handed her a towel, which she wound around her thigh, tying it off at the back. He then held up a Phillip's head screwdriver and what looked like a meat tenderizer.

"No hammer, huh?"

He shook his head. "I looked everywhere. This was the closest I could find, but I think it'll work. It has a nice heft to it."

He passed it to Clare, and she had to admit, it was heavier than she'd been expecting. The head was a burnished silver, the handle wooden with a rubberized grip.

"How's Linda?" she asked, her eyes not leaving the mallet as if it were a talisman that had mesmerized her.

"Sleeping like a baby. Well, like a baby who was bashed over the head with a closet rod. Her breathing seems steady, and the bleeding has stopped at least. I'm no doctor, but I think she'll be okay."

Clare nodded, and finally looked up at Patrick. "What are we going to do about her?"

"What do you mean?" he asked, but she could tell by the way he cut his eyes that he knew exactly what she meant.

"If we do manage to break through the window and get out of this house, are we just going to leave her here?"

Patrick took a moment before he spoke, and in that moment she could see a war in his eyes. He, too, recognized the sound of the ticking clock that urged them to hurry, that warned time was running short, but he also knew her question was a serious one and necessitated a thoughtful answer.

"Clare," he started, "we can't possibly carry her down from here, and even if we could, we don't know how long we'll have to go before we find help. And when she regains consciousness, she'll fight us again. You know I'm right."

He was right, because she did know he was right. Of course, that didn't make the knowledge any easier to swallow.

Patrick reached out and took her hand. "I know it sucks, but I can't see any other way. As soon as we find help, we'll send the police and paramedics out here first thing. I promise."

Clare thought about the poor woman, the torture she'd been through, the insanity she'd wrapped around her mind to protect herself from even greater insanity. She was broken, and Clare had such a need to put her back together again. But like all the king's horses and all the king's men, she had to face the fact that such reconstruction was beyond her abilities.

"Okay," she said, giving him back the mallet. "None of that even matters if we don't get through that damn window."

Their progress back to the window was slow. *Slow and steady*, Clare thought as she crawled over the wood, moving at a snail's pace for fear of breaking through again. They reached their destination without incident. Clare scooted over to one side of the window while Patrick knelt right in front of it. He held the screwdriver so that the tip pressed against the glass at its center, and in the other hand brought the meat tenderizer back. He pounded the handle with the mallet, but the tip only skidded along the glass with a nails-on-the-chalkboard *screech* that made Clare grit her teeth and wince. Patrick tried again with the same result, succeeding only in making a faint scratch across the surface, a literal scratching of the surface.

"I'm going to need your help," he said, holding the screwdriver out toward Clare. "It's hard for me to hold it steady. Maybe if you can hold it two-handed, it'll stay in place when I hit it."

Clare hesitated. The mallet may not be as heavy as a hammer, but it was still plenty heavy. The base of the screwdriver's handle was larger around than a nickel, but not as large as a quarter. If Patrick missed and hit her hand instead . . .

Sensing her thoughts, he said, "I'll be careful, I promise."

Clare blew air through her lips, causing them to flap and make a playing-cards-in-bicycle-spokes sputtering, and took the screwdriver. "If you're too careful, we'll never get out of here. Put all you've got into it, just please try to *aim* as best you can."

"Deal. I don't want to hurt you anymore than you want to be hurt."

Of course, if he did slip and hit her hand, he might feel terrible about it in an abstract way, but she'd feel terrible about it in an actual shattered fingers and passing out from the pain sort of way. She didn't say this, however. It didn't need to be said. They both knew it, as they also both knew it had to be done.

Clare held the screwdriver in place, gripping it with both hands, bracing against the wall to steady herself. Patrick took his time, also gripping the mallet with both hands, taking a few practice swings without actually making contact. Finally he looked at her gravely and nodded. She nodded back then squeezed her eyes shut. She felt the impact of the mallet before she heard it, and sweet relief flooded through her when she realized her fingers were all still intact. Also, she'd managed to hold the screwdriver more or less steady. She opened her eyes and hoped to see a spider web of cracks fissuring the glass. Instead she saw nothing but the most infinitesimal indention under the tip.

"Think it's going to take a little more work," Patrick said with a half-hearted smile.

"Then hit it again, Sam."

Patrick did hit it again. And again. And again. Clare kept expecting him to miss one of these times, but his aim was true, and her hands were surprisingly steady. The indention grew as the screwdriver chipped a groove in the glass, making it easier for her to hold in place. At some point, he told her she could let go and he again held the screwdriver with one hand and beat at it with the other. Tiny cracks began to spread out in a circular pattern around the impact point, widening and lengthening as Patrick continued the assault with the meat tenderizer.

Clare wasn't sure how long he kept it up, maybe five minutes, maybe fifteen, but with one final whack the tip of the screwdriver popped out of the other side of the glass and the entire shaft slid through until the larger base stopped it. At the same instant, the cracks spread like lightning, branching across the entire window's surface, a triangular chunk near the top actually coming lose and falling to the floor, where it shattered into several even smaller pieces.

They both stood staring down at the jagged shards for several minutes as if they couldn't quite believe it. If Clare was completely honest with herself, she hadn't really believed it was going to work. Now, as she stared down at the glass, twinkling dimly in the dull hazy light, a bourgeoning excitement began to flutter in her stomach. She closed her eyes and could smell her father's cologne, hear the sound of her mother humming to herself as she did the dishes, feel the softness of her own bed, taste her father's famous four-alarm fire chili, see Hank's sexy, shy smile. Freedom hadn't felt so close since she first woke up in the basement.

When she opened her eyes again, she saw Patrick pick up the beam and swing it at the window like a bat. It connected with the base of the screw driver and caused the entire round sheet of glass to buckle outward from the center, making a vague cone shape. He hit it again and the glass came loose from the sill completely and fell in an almost solid sheet, landing on the porch overhang with a crash. A few chunks of glass clung to the sill in places, looking like rotten, cracked teeth in a mouth rounded with surprise.

That mouth exhaled a cool breath, the air buffeting Clare's face. It was like the caress of a mother, of a lover, everything soothing and comforting. She moaned softly and stepped forward toward the window.

"Careful of the glass," Patrick said.

Clare didn't acknowledge his warning, but she did watch where she put her hands on the sill as she leaned forward and stuck her head out into the open air. She inhaled a lungful, moaning again, as if she'd never before tasted the sweet nectar of oxygen.

Patrick stepped up behind her and placed a hand on her shoulder. "Let me go first."

Clare glanced downward and saw that the overhang below them was covered in shattered glass. Looked dangerous, but then again, everything about this situation was dangerous. Couldn't really qualify any one thing as more dangerous than any other.

She stepped aside, and Patrick used the beam to knock out the remaining chunks of glass clinging to the sill. He cleared the opening as best he could then turned to Clare. "Can I use that towel?"

She looked down at her leg, the towel wrapped around her thigh like a makeshift bandage. She untied it, noting only a few smears of blood, and gave it to Patrick. He draped it across the bottom of the windowsill then tossed the beam and the rod out the window. They both cleared the overhang and landed in the dirt in front of the house. Patrick put his hands to either side of the window, stepping up and lowering himself down, so that he was sitting on the sill with his legs hanging out. Moving slowly, he turned himself over so that he was lying across the towel on his stomach, half-in and half-out of the window. He pushed himself backward until he was completely out the window, dangling from the sill by his hands.

Clare realized she had stopped breathing and sucked in a breath. She wanted to tell Patrick to come back inside, it was too risky, the overhang might be rotten, but she didn't because she wanted *not* to tell him more. He knew the risks as well as she, but he was willing to take them and she was willing to let him. She stood close to the window and met his gaze when he looked up at her. He seemed about to say something, but then he let go of the sill and dropped.

She let out a tiny squeak and stuck her head out the window. She watched Patrick fall the short distance to the overhang, saying a silent prayer that he wouldn't crash right through. He landed on his feet, but then toppled onto his back. She heard the crunch as he landed on the glass.

"Are you okay?" she called down.

Patrick sat up, and she could see blood on his hands. Then he reached behind him and yanked a large sliver of glass out of his left shoulder blade. "A little cut up, but nothing serious. Hold on a second."

He proceeded to gather up glass shards and toss them over the side of the overhang, sometimes kicking them over. When he was done, having cleared most of the debris away, he looked up. "Okay, come on down. I'll catch you."

Clare realized she was shaking, and her sweat covered her entire body as if she were in a sauna. She knew it was only fear, and some old dead guy had once said that you didn't have to be afraid of fear, or fear was the only thing to be afraid of, or some bit of nonsense she had never fully understood.

Moving before the fear had time to grow and expand, she mimicked what she'd watched Patrick do a moment before until she too was dangling from the sill. She heard him under her, calling her name, urging her to let go, but still she clung to the sill as if her life depended on it.

Ridiculous really. It wasn't that far of a drop, she

knew now that the overhang was sturdy , the glass had been removed, and Patrick was there for her. Yet she remained frozen. Her mind flashed on footage of 9/11 Mr. Brinkley had shown them in history class, people climbing out of windows a hundred stories up to escape the heat of the fire, holding on for as long as they could before plummeting to their deaths.

But she wasn't a hundred stories up. She could actually feel Patrick's hands gripping her ankles, and he continued to talk to her. She was too freaked out to make out his actual words, but she could tell by the tone and cadence he was trying to be soothing, to coax her down.

Damn it, Clare! You're being foolish, and you're wasting precious time. Just let go, open your fingers and—

She let go. The fall lasted not even three seconds. She landed on her feet and also started to topple backward, but Patrick was there to hold her upright.

"See, that wasn't so bad, was it?" he said as she steadied herself.

"Sorry I panicked there for a minute."

"Hey, you're doing great under the circumstances. You're a regular Katniss Everdeen."

Clare laughed. "Does that make you Peeta Mellark?"

He returned her laugh then grimaced with pain.

Clare took his hands and looked at them. A few superficial lacerations and one rather deep slice in the pad of his right thumb. She saw little pieces of glass poking out at various places and began picking them out.

"We don't have time for that right now," he said,

gently pulling his hands away. "Let's get the hell out of here first, and worry about licking our wounds later."

He turned away from her and she saw where the shard had stabbed into his shoulder blade. A crimson stain was spreading across the back of his shirt. He was going to need to have someone look at that, maybe get stitches, but he was right. There was nothing they could do about that at the moment.

She waited as he first got down on his knees and then flat onto his belly, pushing himself backwards until he was hinged at the waist, legs hanging down, torso still on the overhang. He continued to push back until he was once again hanging from a precipice by his fingertips. This drop was a little longer, but not by much. Clare saw him hit the ground with knees bent, tuck into a roll, then come up on his feet. A landing worthy of an Olympic athlete. She actually clapped and whistled.

He made a comedic bow with a flourish of one of his bleeding hands then said, "Okay, Katniss, your turn."

Clare didn't hesitate this time. Her descent wasn't as graceful, but she landed without injury. She lay on the ground for a moment, looking up at the overcast sky, her fingers trailing through the dirt.

Outside! It had been so very long since she'd been outside. She'd actually begun to believe she'd never be outside again.

A darker shadow fell across her vision, and she looked up to see Patrick standing over her, extending a hand.

"Let's go," he said. "It's time to get the hell out of Dodge."

CHAPTER TWENTY-TWO:
THROUGH THE WOODS

PATRICK AND CLARE started down the dirt road toward the wooded area, he with the rod in his hands and her with the beam. They didn't really discuss it, but Patrick certainly wasn't ready to get rid of his weapon and even wished he'd thought to bring along the knife from the kitchen as well. He wouldn't feel safe until they were sitting in a police station, telling their story to a room full of officers.

Only that wasn't the truth. He would possibly never feel safe again. He may always want a weapon handy wherever he went, even in his own home.

Just as they reached the tree line, the path stretching under the overhanging branches to give the impression of entering a tunnel, Clare said, "Maybe we should get off the road. You know, in case Big Daddy comes back."

"Good idea, but let's stay close enough that we can sort of see the road. I'd hate for us to get turned around and lost in the woods."

They walked a few feet into the trees then started forward again, moving parallel to the road. Leaves, twigs, and acorns crunched under their feet, and because of the cloud cover the sky looked very close, like a dropped ceiling. It made Patrick feel vaguely claustrophobic even though they were finally out in the open. They walked in silence for a few more minutes before Clare spoke again.

"Where do you think we are?"

Patrick looked around, taking in the firs, pine trees, evergreens, even a few oaks. Trees common for the area that you could find almost anywhere. "It's hard to say. Thinking logically, he took you and Linda from Greer and me from Greenville, so somewhere in that vicinity, maybe between the two cities. Wherever we are, it's way the hell out in the country, that's for sure."

"Should we, I don't know, just start shouting for help or something? I mean, it seems like we're in the middle of nowhere, but maybe there's another house just on the other side of these trees."

Patrick came to a halt, his feet kicking up dust and dead leaves. He hadn't thought of that, it seemed too simple he supposed. Plus, if they started screaming and their abductor was nearby, he would hear them and know they had escaped. Then again, if he was nearby, why would he have left them alone for so long? Hard to speculate on the workings of a psychotic mind.

This psycho, Big Daddy as he had told Clare to call him, was a menacing but largely faceless presence that loomed in Patrick's mind. He had seen the guy in the Furman parking lot by the lake for a few seconds before being bashed in the head with the bat, but when Patrick tried to picture him, he found it nearly impossible. Just a jumble of disparate features that he couldn't quite fit together to make a cohesive whole.

Big Daddy was a shadow figure, a wraith that haunted Patrick's thoughts like some musty ghost stalking the halls of a decrepit mansion. That somehow made this situation even worse as his abductor took on mythic proportions in his imagination.

"Well," Clare prompted, pulling him out of his reverie. "What do you say?"

He considered it another moment then shrugged. "What the hell? It's worth a shot."

They spent the next five minutes shouting for help. They shouted until Patrick's throat felt raw and scratchy. Once they quieted, they stood still, both with their heads slightly tilted, listening for some sound, some indication that they had been heard. Maybe someone calling back, maybe footsteps running their way.

There was nothing. Not entirely true. The chirping of birds in the trees, the twittering of squirrels, the creaky music made by branches swaying in the breeze, even the distant otherworldly hum of an airplane somewhere overhead. How he wished he was on that plane, destination anywhere but here.

"Guess that was a waste of time," Clare said, a blush of embarrassment coloring her cheeks.

"Like I said, it was worth a shot. Let's keep going. Further we get from that house, the better I'll feel."

They continued on, unconsciously matching one another's pace, walking so close that at times their arms occasionally brushed. Patrick felt even tenser now than inside the house, his stomach cramping and his posture rigid, jerking at every rustle of leaves or twitter of bird. The outdoors seemed somehow menacing to him, and it wasn't just that the day was gray with wisps of patchy fog drifting between the trees, making the woods seem like the location of some horror movie. *Son of the Blair Witch*, something cheesy like that. That was part of it, but it wasn't all of it. Another element was that despite being outside, they seemed more isolated than ever. Their screaming jag had brought that down like a hammer blow. They were free of the house, but they weren't free yet. They were simply in a larger cell.

Next to him, Clare slowed her pace then stopped, and he stopped with her. She crossed her arms tightly across her chest and her gaze flittered like a butterfly, never landing on his own eyes.

"What's the matter?" he asked.

She stared down at the ground then said in a near-whisper, "I need to pee."

"Oh, is that all? Well, just go into the trees a little ways then. I'll wait."

She glanced over her shoulder, looking deeper into the woods before looking back at him. She didn't have to say anything for him to know what she was thinking. She didn't want them to split up, not even for a moment. He knew, because he felt it too. They were life preservers for one another, and one didn't want to let go of his or her life preserver even for a moment because it only takes a moment to drown.

"It's okay," he said with more confidence than he felt. "I'll stay right here but with my back turned. You just go a few feet, maybe behind that clump of bushes over there."

She glanced at the bushes in question. "You promise you won't move?"

"I'll stand right in this spot until you get back."

With a nod, she started off into the woods and Patrick turned to face the dirt path. He let his mind drift. His thoughts circled his family, school, but mostly they focused on Robert. Though it had only been a matter of days since Patrick's abduction, he felt as if he hadn't seen his boyfriend in weeks. Maybe months. He missed everything about Robert. His smile, his laugh, the way his hair always looked slightly messy even right after combing it, even his smell. Sometimes when they lay together watching TV, Patrick would bury his nose in Robert's hair and inhale the man's scent. Patrick couldn't define that scent—he'd never smelled anything else quite like it. It was unique to Robert, like an olfactory fingerprint.

Patrick wanted more than anything else in the world to lie in Robert's arms again, to breathe in his distinctive aroma. That was what kept him fighting, the motivation behind everything he'd done since waking up in that dank cell. Robert was the carrot dangling in front of him.

When he felt a hand on his shoulder, Patrick let out a startled shout and spun around with the raised rod.

Clare stood there, staring at him with wide eyes for a moment before she broke into laughter. After a few seconds, Patrick joined her.

"Sorry," she said between giggles. "Didn't mean to scare you."

"My fault. I got lost in my own head."

They started walking again, Clare letting the beam drag along behind her, creating a trail through the dirt in their wake.

"So what were you thinking about?" she asked.

"When?"

"When you were lost in your head."

"Oh, just how good it will be to see my boyfriend again."

Clare was silent for a moment then said, "So . . . you're gay then?"

"Yeah." He snuck a peek at her from the corner of her eye. "That's not a problem, is it?"

"Of course not," she said quickly. "I'm a member of the Gay-Straight Student Alliance at school, and I'm friendly with a couple of the guys in drama club."

"So, some of your best friends are gay, is that what you're saying?"

She glanced over at him, and when she saw his smile, she smiled in return. "No, smart-ass. I didn't say they were my best friends, but I don't have a problem with gay people."

"Okay, you just had this look of disappointment on your face, that's all."

She blushed and looked away from him. He knew the score. She had a schoolgirl crush on him, which was understandable, and he really shouldn't tease her this way, but it felt good. It felt *normal*. His tension eased with the normality of it.

Clare abruptly stopped again. "Don't tell me you have to pee again already," he said.

She didn't respond to that jest, but pointed straight ahead. "Do I see what I think I see, or is it a mirage or something?"

He followed her finger out through the trees in front of them but didn't see anything. At first. Then he lowered his gaze and he did. About a hundred yards, through the foliage, he could see a road. *A paved road.*

An excitement expanded inside him like a hot air

balloon. He tried to temper the excitement by reminding himself that they weren't out of the woods yet, figuratively speaking. A road, yes, which was a sign of civilization and could lead them to help, but he had no way of knowing how many miles they might have to walk before finding a gas station or another house. Plus, being so far off the beaten path as they were, there wasn't likely to be much traffic on this road.

Even as this thought went through his mind, his ears detected the hum of tires on pavement and the low growl of an approaching engine. At first he assumed he was imagining it, an auditory hallucination, wishful thinking, but then Clare perked up next to him.

"Do you hear that?" she said then without waiting for a response, she took off at a sprint toward the road.

"Clare, wait!" Patrick shouted then started after her. He made it only two steps, however, before his foot caught on a gnarled root hidden by a carpet of decaying leaves. He fell straight forward, banging his chin on the ground, the rod skittering away. He pushed up to his hands and knees, blood dribbling from his lip to patter into the dirt. His ankle throbbed and seemed to be swelling in his sock. Not broken, but possibly sprained.

As he held onto a tree trunk to pull himself to his feet, he spotted Clare breaking through the woods, almost to the road. He limped after her, pain flaring in his ankle. His eyes were locked on the ground before him to make sure he didn't trip again and hurt himself further. He heard the sound of a vehicle getting closer, and Clare shouting, and then he heard the sound of an impact and the screech of brakes.

His head shot up. He'd covered half the distance to the road, and he could see Clare lying on her back in the road, her head turned away from him, an SUV stopped diagonally, its front end hanging over a ditch on the far side of the road.

Patrick picked up his pace, hobbling on the wounded ankle but gritting his teeth against the pain. Ahead, he saw the wooden beam where Clare had apparently dropped it, and he snatched it up, using it like a crutch.

As he made his way onto the pavement, the door to the SUV opened and an older gentleman in a rumpled button-up shirt and wrinkled khaki pants stepped out, his expression dazed and a little lost, as if he didn't quite know where he was or what was happening.

Clare, in her excitement, must have run right out in front of the car. In such an isolated area, the driver probably wasn't expecting anyone to come tearing out of the woods, and he hit her before he could stop.

Sparing the driver only the most cursory glance, Patrick let the beam drop to the pavement and knelt next to Clare. Blood was pooling beneath her head, and her head seemed turned too far. He felt vomit surge into his mouth when he saw the fractured bone poking up through her pants leg about halfway between knee and ankle. Her eyes were open and vacant. He reached for her arm and felt for a pulse in her wrist. He wasn't terribly surprised when he didn't find one.

"Do you know CPR?" he called to the driver, not taking his eyes off of Clare. Her empty stare into nothingness was almost mesmerizing. When he received no answer from the man, the bastard was probably in shock himself, he said again, "Do you know CRP? And if you have a cell phone, call 911. We need help, please!"

Still no answer, but he heard the man's footsteps on the pavement, stopping just behind him, then a minute *click*. Patrick's core temperature dropped suddenly, as if he'd been dunked in ice water, and he turned slowly. The first thing he saw was the gun, the barrel pointed at his head, and then his gaze rose to the man's face.

The puzzle pieces came together in his memory and he recognized this face. Just as he now recognized the SUV as the one he'd seen idling in the parking lot at Furman.

Big Daddy was home.

CHAPTER TWENTY-THREE:
DADDY'S HOME

"**YOU TWO HAVE** been naughty children," the man said, his voice calm, even a bit chipper as if he and Patrick were engaged in a pleasant chat. "Where's your mother?"

At first, Patrick couldn't move, couldn't speak. He stared at the gun as if hypnotized by it. The opening at the end of the barrel seemed so small yet so large at the same time. It was hard to believe that a projectile propelled out of that hole could cause so much destruction. Patrick had gotten into a few scrapes and physical altercations in his life, but until this moment he'd never had a gun pointed at him. Not even a cap gun when he was a child, as far as he could remember. He found the experience utterly debilitating.

Big Daddy smiled, not a menacing smile, but again one that looked almost congenial. "I could tell you were going to be a feisty one from the first time I saw you running. So much energy and stamina. A boy a father could be proud of, if only you turned that energy to something constructive. Instead, I see you've been a very bad influence on your sister. Shame, she was shaping up to be such an obedient girl. You led her astray and look what happened. Doesn't pay to misbehave."

Patrick opened his mouth, wanting to curse the sadistic bastard, to unleash a tirade of venom at this monster in a man suit, but what came out was an absurd question. "Where've you been?"

"Sorry, son, got unavoidably detained. Would you believe this is the second person I've hit with my car in the last few days?"

Though the question Patrick asked was ridiculous given the circumstances, the mere act of speaking seemed to break his mental paralysis and the wheels in his mind began turning again. Clare was dead. Tragic, heartbreaking, but he couldn't let it cripple him or he'd end up dead as well. He had to push the grief aside, something to be taken at and felt later when he had the luxury. Right now, he needed to go into survival mode, and that meant doing and saying whatever he had to, in order to get out of this alive.

"It wasn't me," he said, and he didn't have to try too hard to make his voice sound subservient and plaintive. "I swear. I wanted to stay where you put me, but Clare insisted. I didn't want to leave the house, but when she went I felt like I had to go with her. You know, to look out for her. That's what big brothers do."

The gun didn't waver, but the man's expression altered slightly. Became something Patrick thought a writer might call wistful, but also with a certain amount of wary doubt. "That's hard to believe. She had her defiant moments, but she had become such a good girl."

"It was an act," Patrick said, working to keep the

desperation out of his tone. He didn't want to oversell it. "You know how girls can be, saying one thing when they mean another. Manipulative, especially with their fathers."

The doubt remained on Big Daddy's face, but Patrick could only hope it was switching from doubt about him to doubt about Clare. He felt horrible throwing her under the bus like this, but he'd never have done it if she hadn't been beyond caring. Things couldn't get any worse for her at this point. A horrible truth, but a truth nonetheless.

"Girls can be a handful," the man said thoughtfully. "I remember my older sister was always getting into trouble, but our dad thought she was a perfect princess. Had him snowed, as they say. But I knew she would climb out her bedroom window at night and go gallivanting around with boys, drinking and smoking dope and screwing around. Got herself knocked up at the age of fourteen. Broke our poor daddy's heart."

Patrick watched Big Daddy carefully, looking for his moment, but despite the man taking a detour down memory lane, his focus remained on Patrick and the gun remained pointed directly at him.

"She said she was going to meet some boy," Patrick said, not knowing how deep this man's madness went, but hoping he could play into it without tipping his hand. "I tried to talk her out of it, but when I realized she couldn't be dissuaded I figured it would be safer if I went with her to keep her out of serious trouble. I thought it would be what you'd want me to do."

The man's gaze drifted away from Patrick and down to Clare's prone body. The barrel of the gun dropped as well, not much but it veered down and slightly off to the left. Not a perfect opportunity, but Patrick realized it may be the only one he got. Moving swiftly, he hefted the beam and swung it toward the man's hand. Big Daddy's eyes snapped back to Patrick and he started to raise the gun again, but then the beam struck his hand.

The gun went off, and Patrick fully expected to feel the bullet rip into his chest, but instead it sparked off the pavement next to him. The gun dropped to the cement, and Big Daddy immediately bent and reached for it. Patrick used the beam like a hockey stick and sent the gun skittering into the trees.

With a growl, Big Daddy leapt at him.

Patrick tried to lash out with the beam, but the older man was surprisingly quick and was on him before he could get it around. He tackled Patrick, and the two men toppled backward onto the pavement, the beam pinned between them. Big Daddy's strong callused hands wrapped around his throat and started to squeeze. Patrick felt his windpipe constricting, the airflow cutting off, and he began to buck and twist and writhe, Big Daddy on top of him and riding him like a mechanical bull.

"Shh, just go to sleep," the older man whispered directly into Patrick's face. "Daddy doesn't want to hurt you. Just go to sleep and we can decide your punishment later."

Patrick tried to get an arm up to strike at Big Daddy, but he found that the beam was in his way. After more wiggling, straining to get even the tiniest stream of oxygen into his lungs, he freed his left arm and landed a glancing blow to Big Daddy's right ear.

The man reacted by backhanding Patrick in the

face, a blow right across the cheekbone. Hurt like a sonofabitch, but it meant that Big Daddy loosened his stranglehold. Patrick seized the opportunity and pushed up on the beam as if he were bench pressing a barbell. It lifted the older man and Patrick wrenched to the side, tossing Big Daddy off him. Unfortunately, he lost his grip on the wooden beam and it was tossed aside as well.

Wasting no time, Patrick leapt to his feet and bolted for the car. In his mind he bolted, anyway. His injured ankle made the reality of his flight more of a lumbering lurch. The SUV was only a few feet away, but that distance seemed to stretch like a collapsible telescope being pulled out to its full length. He could imagine Big Daddy behind him, rushing up with the beam in hand, ready to clobber him over the back of the head.

Patrick didn't glance over his shoulder to see if what he imagined were actually about to happen; it would have only slowed him down even further. One small bit of luck that came down in his favor was that Big Daddy had left the driver's side door open when he'd gotten out of the car. Patrick reached it without being clubbed, and dove inside, shutting the door behind him and hitting the lock. Looking through the window, he discovered that the older man wasn't as close as Patrick had feared, but still only a couple of seconds behind. Big Daddy reached the door and began tugging on the handle.

Patrick reached for the ignition, his fingers closing on nothing. He'd hoped that if Big Daddy had not had the presence of mind to close the car door then he might not have had the presence of mind to take the keys out of the ignition. Apparently that was too much to hope for.

As if to drive the point home, he heard a tinkling and glanced out the driver's side window once again. Big Daddy stood there, a teasing smile curling his lips. The keys dangled from an upheld hand.

"Every minute of disobedience only increases your punishment," the older man said, a touch of what sounded like sincere sorrow in his voice. "But you are bringing this on yourself."

Big Daddy bent to place the key in the lock, and Patrick scrambled across the seat, unlocking and popping open the passenger's side door in almost one motion, tumbling out into the ditch that ran the side of the road. Stagnant rain water seeped into his clothes, smelling vaguely of sewage. He clambered up into the trees on the other side of the road and began his limping run through the woods. In his current condition, he couldn't hope to outrun Big Daddy, but maybe he could outmaneuver him, lose him in the foliage.

Patrick zigged and zagged, changing course at random, panting and puffing like he never had when taking his runs around campus. Up ahead, he heard a roar, and his mind registered what the sound indicated even before he burst out of the trees and skidded to a halt on the shore of a fast-flowing river.

He stood for a moment, wondering if this was some branch of the Reedy River, which fed the lake back at Furman, though it didn't really matter. He could attempt to swim across, or turn right or left.

Before he could make a decision, he heard the crunch of leaves and twigs behind him and turned to find Big Daddy coming out of the tree line, once again holding the gun and training it on Patrick.

"Not as swift as I remember," the man said. He was out of breath as well, sweat glistening on his face, but his expression was triumphant and energized. "Guess you must have hurt yourself or something. I had time to go back, find the gun, and still got here just behind you."

Patrick held out his hands in an imploring gesture. "Look, Dad, just let me—"

"Don't," Big Daddy said. His voice was soft but full of authority, and Patrick immediately went silent. "Don't play the dutiful son act with me. You already played that card; won't work again. Poor little Clare. You probably did lead her astray, maybe even forced her to leave the house against her will. Is that why she ran out into the road like that? Was she running from you? Whatever happened, her blood is on your hands as much as if you had plunged a knife right into her heart. Get on your knees."

Patrick started to cry. He couldn't help it, the tears just poured as if from an open faucet. "Please, just . . . please."

He couldn't think of a more elegant plea for his life, so he kept repeating the word *please*.

Big Daddy stepped forward and placed the barrel of the gun against the center of Patrick's forehead. It felt as if were burning a circle in his flesh. He knew that could only be psychosomatic, but it didn't stop him from wincing at the heat.

"Get on your knees," the older man said again, and now there were no traces of warmth or mirth. The voice was flat, cold, merciless.

Patrick briefly considered allowing himself to fall backward into the rushing waters, trying to swim away before Big Daddy could get off a shot. It seemed unlikely, and he felt all the energy and will drain from his body and he slipped down to his knees. The only name he could put to the feeling of surrender that washed over him was *resignation*. It terrified him, but if he were honest, he'd have to admit it also felt sort of good.

He closed his eyes and waited to feel the impact of the bullet. Only instead of a bullet, what he felt was the butt of the gun against the back of his head.

CHAPTER TWENTY-FOUR:
PUTTING SIS TO BED

PATRICK AWOKE TO the roar of the ocean crashing on a rocky shore, thunder booming in the tumultuous heavens, nuclear missiles detonating right next to his ear. The sounds of apocalypse, of annihilation, of volcanos erupting fire into the sky and worlds imploding.

He tried to raise his arms to cover his ears with his hands, but he found his arms would not move. As he listened to the cataclysmic roar ebb and flow, he realized it would do no good anyway. The sound was not without but within, inside his own throbbing head.

He opened his eyes and winced at the glare of light that stabbed into his corneas. His throat was scratchy, his tongue a dried-out sponge lying abandoned in his mouth. Something covered his mouth, something sticky that sealed his lips together. His face was on the ground, turned to the side, and he felt some kind of grid digging into his cheek. He tried again to move his arms, which were pulled behind his back. He glanced over his shoulder, straining his neck, and found his hands duct taped together. His feet were likewise secured with tape at the ankles.

The noise in his skull began to subside, though pain still cut across his cranium like broken glass grinding into his brain, and he became aware of another sound. This one was *without*. A solid *thunk* followed by an almost musical cascade like a light hail. He looked straight ahead again, squinting against the light, looking at the world through a series rusty metal squares. Glancing upward, the blue sky—the cloud cover and mist seemed to have burned off—visible through the branches was likewise cut into these squares.

Though he found it hard to think through the pain, one stray thought snuck through. *The dog kennel. The one in the attic.*

That one thought seemed to create enough of an opening for others to make it through.

He assembled the kennel and stuck me in it. Hands and feet duct taped, and it's probably a strip of duct tape over my mouth. But why does he have me outside?

He turned his head to the right, seeking out the source of the *thunk*/cascade. His abductor was about a yard away, using a shovel to dig a hole. The *thunk* as he planted the blade in the ground with a foot, the cascade as he tossed the dirt to the side where it formed a mound like a giant anthill. Lying just behind him was Clare.

No, not Clare. Not her strength or her humor or her anxiety. None of the essential things that had made her *her*. This was just her body, an empty vessel which had been empty of its vital contents. A hollow shell. A dummy, a doll, a mannequin with Clare's face. Thinking of it that way was all that kept him from completely breaking down, though tears slid down either side of his face as if racing to throw themselves off his chin. Salty, competitive lemmings.

As Patrick watched, Linda suddenly danced into view. Literally *danced*. She twirled and leapt, her faded pink nightgown ballooning around her. Her feet were bare and filthy as she stepped lightly toward the older man and held out a hand. "Dance with me, Big Daddy. I've missed you so."

Big Daddy paused in his shoveling, leaning on the handle as if it were all that kept him upright. His face was red, like a beet sitting on the stalk of his neck, and sweat coated his face and dampened his shirt so that it clung to his torso. He sighed heavily, an exhale of weary exasperation. "I knew I should have left you in the house," he said. "Just be quiet and stay out of my way until I'm done. I still have a lot of work to do."

The woman clutched her hands to her chest and ducked her head down as if expecting to be struck. Patrick thought she looked emotionally stung. No, crushed, the way you'd look if the person you loved most in the world told you they'd never even liked you a little.

"Don't be mad at me, Big Daddy. I tried to stop them, really I did, but the boy hit me in the head. I don't think he—"

As she spoke, Linda glanced his way and paused when she saw he was conscious and staring back at her. Her expression changed again, her features twisting into a mask of rage. She stalked forward, moving quickly, and kicked out at the kennel, making it shake, rust flaking down to land in Patrick's hair like dandruff.

"You ungrateful little shit!" she yelled, her hands clenched into tight fists. "Big Daddy has given us a lovely home, protects us and keeps us safe, and how do you thank him? By bashing me over the head and running off with your sister. Well, see where that got you? Just look what you've done to your sister. *Just look*!"

"Enough!" Big Daddy shouted, and Linda immediately quieted and ducked her head down again. A subservient posture. "Linda, you go on back to the house now."

"I don't want to go back to the house," she whined, like a petulant child. "This is the first time I've been outside in ages. Let me stay. I can help."

"You can help by going back to the house. I need to have a man to man talk with the boy, *alone*. You don't have to go inside, just wait for me in the front yard. Be careful of the glass."

Linda hesitated another minute, and then with a final kick to the kennel, she ran off through the woods.

Patrick and his abductor stared at one another in silence for several moments, Patrick trussed up in the kennel while Big Daddy continued to lean on the shovel, his lips forming a gentle smile. A *fatherly* smile.

"You almost gave me a heart attack, boy," the man said at last, resuming his shoveling. "I had to chase after you, and then haul your ass all the way back to the road, get you and your sister in the car. Then I had to crawl up into the attic and haul out the kennel, and now I'm playing grave digger. I'm a little old for all this exertion."

Patrick wiggled around, the unpadded bottom of

the cage pressing uncomfortably into his chest and thighs. He moved his hands as much as he could, hoping to loosen the tape enough to free himself. The tape held firm.

"You really trashed the house," Big Daddy went on, focused on his work and not looking up at Patrick. "And you killed Spike. I've had that dog for several years, and he was a great family pet. I have to say, after seeing what you did to him, I was so pissed off, I considered throwing you in this hole and burying you with your sister."

Patrick began wrenching his hands harder, but the tape was sturdy and wound around several times.

"Calm down," Big Daddy said, tossing a shovel-full of dirt in his direction. Some of it pelted Patrick in the face. "I've had some time to cool off, think about this rationally. You will need to be punished. What kind of father would I be if I didn't teach you there were consequences for your bad behavior? But if I were being completely honest, this isn't entirely your fault. This is what happens when children are left unsupervised for long periods of time. I have to take my share of the blame for leaving you alone for so long. I mean, yes, your mother was here, but I think we both know she can't be counted on to be disciplinarian."

Closing his eyes, Patrick willed his breathing to slow and he considered his options. He had gotten over every barrier keeping him prisoner in that house; he should be able to get out of this situation. The kennel was old and rusted; a few strong kicks would probably be all it took to knock one of the sides loose. Of course, as soon as he started kicking, Big Daddy would be over here in a shot. And even if he did manage to worm his way out, it wasn't as if he could get very far with his ankles strapped together.

Patrick opened his eyes and saw that Big Daddy had paused his digging again, fixing him with an intense stare.

"I never meant to be gone so long," he said in a tone that seemed to plead for forgiveness. "You have to believe that. I wanted to be here when you woke up, to help you start getting acclimated to your new home. I just needed to run to the store and pick up a few supplies. Should have been there and back in less than an hour, easy-peasy, but unfortunately fate intervened. I ended up hitting a man with my car in the Walmart parking lot. He ran right out in front of me before I could stop. Real sad sap kind of a guy, no family, just a bunch of dogs from what I understand.

"I didn't kill him, but messed him up pretty good, put him into a coma. And as if that weren't bad enough, turns out I had some unpaid parking tickets and a suspended license. No one to blame there but my own absent-mindedness and procrastination. That meant there was suddenly a lot of scrutiny on me, and I couldn't risk coming back here and having someone discover our little sanctuary. This old house has been in my family for generations, but I keep a little apartment near downtown Greer. I stuck close to there until I felt the heat was off me. Paid my fines, got my license reinstated, and that sap I hit even woke up. So now I'm home, and you're going to get the structure and discipline you need. We're going to be a family."

Big Daddy continued shoveling until he had made a narrow trench, not the standard six feet deep but then again this wasn't a standard burial. The man kneeled down next to Clare's body, said a few words too soft for Patrick to make out, kissed the girl on the forehead, then rolled her into the shallow grave.

Hot tears squeezing from his eyes, Patrick screamed out all his rage at the injustice of this, the sound muffled by the thick tape over his mouth. So close, they had been so fucking close. Yet close didn't count for much when all was said and done. In fact, it only made it worse.

Big Daddy walked over to the kennel, bending over to stare though the grating at Patrick. "I know you miss your sister. I do too, but don't worry. We'll always remember her fondly, and someday soon, God willing, there will be another to fill the void she left."

As Patrick continued to cry, feeling completely hollowed out as if someone had removed all his internal organs and bones, Big Daddy walked back over to the grave and began shoveling dirt over Clare.

CHAPTER TWENTY-FIVE:
IT'S A GIRL

PATRICK SAT IN the dark, back against the rough stone wall. The lack of light was part of his punishment, as was the fact that he only had the food bucket in the cell with him. Big Daddy would bring the other bucket once a day and watch while Patrick used it. He'd resisted as long as he could, but eventually it had been a choice between using the bucket or fouling his pants and having to sit in his own filth. Humiliating and dehumanizing.

Speaking of which, he reached into the bucket next to him and pulled out a handful of dog food and tossed it into his mouth like popcorn, crunching down on the kibble. The taste was chalky and sour, but he swallowed the mess down with a grimace. He turned the handle of the spigot and gulped several swallows of water.

He had no idea exactly how much time had passed since his escape attempt with Clare. Weeks? Months? It was hard to keep track of time when he was submerged here in total darkness. Long enough for the welts on his back from the first part of his punishment to have mostly healed, and long enough for Big Daddy to have done some remodeling to the basement. He'd completely removed the wall that once separated the two cells, making one long room, and the door on this side, the one Patrick had busted through with the wooden beam, had likewise been removed and the space bricked up.

Patrick had sat in silence, watching as Big Daddy sealed him up brick by brick, spreading globs of mortar and tapping down each brick with fastidious precision. Patrick felt like some character in an Edgar Allan Poe story. All he needed was a black cat perched atop his head.

Of course, there was still the thick door on the far side of the cell. It had seemed impenetrable before, and now it was also unreachable. Another upgrade Big Daddy had made to the cell was drilling a metal ring into the concrete floor, a ring to which Patrick's left ankle was attached with a short length of chain. A semi-circular diameter of three feet, which defined his movements in the cell. Another metal ring had been drilled into the floor on the far side of the cell. Patrick didn't like to think what that signified. Truth be told, he tried not to think of much of anything. It was easier that way.

Patrick gripped the ring with one hand and tugged at it halfheartedly. When he'd first been chained to it, he'd spent hours trying to dislodge it from the floor, but he might as well have been trying to lift a car over his head or uproot a tree with only his bare hand. He'd worked at the manacle on his ankle as well, but a small, sturdy padlock secured the thing and he had been unable to remove it.

Maybe I could gnaw my own foot off. Free myself that way, and I bet my own flesh would taste better than this Alpo.

He laughed at this, a cracked, unhinged sound that might have once disturbed him, but now he was used to it.

Again, he wondered how long he'd been down here in this tomb. Weeks? Months? Longer?

Maybe always. Maybe I've always been here.

This caused him to laugh again, throwing his head back and cackling at the high ceiling. The shadows seemed to swirl around him, a quilt of darkness that enveloped him in its inky embrace. The laughter only ceased when a sound from above caught his ear, a car approaching and then coming to a stop. Big Daddy had gone out earlier—*an hour? two?*— but he seemed to be home again.

Patrick found himself getting excited, hoping that the man had brought back some Snausages. The treats were a bit rubbery but tasted much better than the dry dog food.

A door slammed, sounded like the one in the kitchen, then footsteps tracked slowly down the hall to the basement door. Patrick listened to the heavy tread on the stairs and thought he heard a few grunts of exertion. So, not Snausages but something heavier Big Daddy had brought home from his excursion out. Patrick's mind momentarily strayed to the other metal ring but then veered away again.

When the overhead light blazed to life, Patrick winced, squinted, and held up a hand to shield his eyes from the glare. He'd been in the dark so long, the light felt unnatural and sliced into his brain like a scalpel.

The door at the far end of the cell opened and Big Daddy stepped over the threshold, pausing to lean against the jam and catch his breath. Then he turned, bent at the waist, reaching back into the basement, and began to walk backwards, pulling an unconscious girl into the cell by her sneaker-clad feet.

She was younger than Clare; Patrick could see that right away. If he had to venture a guess, he'd say thirteen or fourteen. She wore a peach blouse with a stylish leather jacket on top of it, and designer jeans. Her hair was a deep black, cut short but with bangs that hung over her eyes like a veil.

After chaining the girl's ankle to the metal ring—her chain seemed to be a bit longer than Patrick's, probably so she could reach the spigot as well—Big Daddy left the room for a moment and then returned with three buckets. He placed two of these by the girl then brought the other one over to Patrick's side of the cell.

A wide grin spread across Big Daddy's face. "We have a new addition to our family. A new sister for you. Our household is complete again, and we're going to be happy."

Patrick looked up at the man and said, "Did you bring any Snausages?"

Reaching down, Big Daddy tousled Patrick's hair then left the cell, closing the door behind him. Patrick heard the thick *clunk* of a bolt sliding into place. Even with the chains and manacles, better safe than sorry.

The light remained on, and with his second bucket being returned, Patrick assumed his punishment was finally over. He smiled gratefully.

He glanced at the girl again. Still except for the

steady rise and fall of her chest. She'd awaken soon, and Patrick would introduce himself. Try to comfort her, explain what was happening, help her adjust to her new familial situation. The sooner she accepted it, the better. He couldn't let her end up like Clare. He had to look out for her, protect her.

After all, what else was a big brother for?

THE END?

Not if you want to dive into more of Crystal Lake Publishing's Tales from the Darkest Depths!

Check out our amazing website and online store. https://www.crystallakepub.com

We always have great new projects and content on the website to dive into, as well as a newsletter, behind the scenes options, social media platforms, and our own dark fiction shared-world series and our very own store. If you use the IGotMyCLPBook! coupon code in the store (at the checkout), you'll get a one-time-only 50% discount on your first eBook purchase!

Our webstore even has categories specifically for KU books, non-fiction, anthologies, and Mark Allan Gunnells himself.

ABOUT THE AUTHOR

Mark Allan Gunnells loves to tell stories. He has since he was a kid, penning one-page tales that were Twilight Zone knockoffs. He likes to think he has gotten a little better since then. He loves reader feedback, and above all he loves telling stories. He lives in Greer, SC, with his husband Craig A. Metcalf.

Since its founding in August 2012, Crystal Lake Publishing has quickly become one of the world's leading publishers of Dark Fiction and Horror books in print, eBook, and audio formats.

While we strive to present only the highest quality fiction and entertainment, we also endeavour to support authors along their writing journey. We offer our time and experience in non-fiction projects, as well as author mentoring and services, at competitive prices.

With several Bram Stoker Award wins and many other wins and nominations, Crystal Lake Publishing puts integrity, honor, and respect at the forefront of our publishing operations.

We strive for each book and outreach program we spearhead to not only entertain and touch or comment on issues that affect our readers, but also to strengthen and support the Dark Fiction field and its authors.

Not only do we find and publish authors we believe are destined for greatness, but we strive to work with men and woman who endeavour to be decent human beings who care more for others than themselves, while still being hard working, driven, and passionate artists and storytellers.

Crystal Lake Publishing is and will always be a beacon of what passion and dedication, combined with overwhelming teamwork and respect, can accomplish. We endeavour to know each and every one of our readers, while building personal relationships with our authors, reviewers, bloggers, podcasters, bookstores, and libraries.

We will be as trustworthy, forthright, and transparent as any business can be, while also keeping most of the headaches away from our authors, since it's our job to solve the problems so they can stay in a creative mind. Which of course also means paying our authors.

We do not just publish books, we present to you worlds within your world, doors within your mind, from talented authors who sacrifice so much for a moment of your time.

There are some amazing small presses out there, and through collaboration and open forums we will continue to support other presses in the goal of helping authors and showing the world what quality small presses are capable of accomplishing. No one wins when a small press goes down, so we will always be there to support hardworking, legitimate presses and their authors. We don't see Crystal Lake as the best press out there, but we will always strive to be the best, strive to be the most interactive and grateful, and even blessed press around. No matter what happens over time, we will also take our mission very seriously while appreciating where we are and enjoying the journey.

What do we offer our authors that they can't do for themselves through self-publishing?

We are big supporters of self-publishing (especially hybrid publishing), if done with care, patience, and planning. However, not every author has the time or inclination to do market research, advertise, and set up book launch strategies. Although a lot of authors are successful in doing it all, strong small presses will always be there for the authors who just want to do what they do best: write.

What we offer is experience, industry knowledge, contacts and trust built up over years. And due to our strong brand and trusting fanbase, every Crystal Lake Publishing book comes with weight of respect. In time our fans begin to trust our judgment and will try a new author purely based on our support of said author.

With each launch we strive to fine-tune our approach, learn from our mistakes, and increase our reach. We continue to assure our authors that we're here for them and that we'll carry the weight of the launch and dealing with third parties while they focus on their strengths—be it writing, interviews, blogs, signings, etc.

We also offer several mentoring packages to authors that include knowledge and skills they can use in both traditional and self-publishing endeavours.

We look forward to launching many new careers.

This is what we believe in. What we stand for. This will be our legacy.

Welcome to Crystal Lake Publishing—Tales from the Darkest Depths

THANK YOU FOR PURCHASING THIS BOOK

9 781637 529911